MW01105040

Tea with the Tiger

Tea with the Tiger

Nathan Unsworth

QUATTRO BOOKS

The publication of *Tea with the Tiger* has been generously supported by
the Canada Council for the Arts and the Ontario Arts Council.

Cover painting: Robert Marra
Cover design: Diane Mascherin
Editor: Luciano Iacobelli
Typography: Grey Wolf Typography

Library and Archives Canada Cataloguing in Publication

Unsworth, Nathan
    Tea with the tiger / Nathan Unsworth.

Issued also in an electronic format.
ISBN 978-1-927443-05-7

    I. Title.

PS8641.N88T43 2012   C813'.6   C2012-903888-1

Published by Quattro Books Inc.
382 College Street
Toronto, Ontario, M5T 1S8
www.quattrobooks.ca

Printed in Canada

For my Mother & Father
and for Dr. Catherine Benes,
a great and thoughtful psychiatrist

PART I:
PROLOGUE

THE SKY IS FILLED with paper clouds like a fax machine erupting; dispensing diaphanous folds of white and Technicolor and faded pink. I imagine, if I blink, the sky will be normal and I will be sane. But I don't blink. I can't. And every time I do, it's moonstruck bats in the belfry; hills brushing down at an artist's stroke, where they are joined at a delusional lake where flowertrees float on witch-grass and rye. They're disconnected like during the flood. To see them perfectly is to recognize this: They really drift. Boy, do they ever. This is not the flood which wiped out the ancients but it is a flood of madness, I think, and if not, then what? I see elephants walking on water, like Salvador Dali has procured my mind, taken leverage with great swaths of colourful paint then spattered it on in a fit of rage.

Why me? Why *oh why* me? This is something I've asked as a child; repeatedly over my pillow while pounding a concave into its centre, like I was trying to beat away memories. Harmful memories which wouldn't depart. I've asked it so much now I'm blue in the face.

Why?

I was a boy from Russia, a Montreal child, a lab rat. I was a stringy teenager with a taste for nature. But I had to be the scapegoat. It had to be me. I've told myself this to justify the pain, but the pain comes and goes like the passing moon. When the moon is full, the pain is great. I must relinquish myself to be a scared thing. But for now the moon is sleeping. For now, the pain is small.

But the madness is real.

That it had to go somewhere was something I believed from a young age, and was going to land here, directly on my small round head like a piano dropping from the 3rd floor, squashing the young man on the pavement, leaving little of him to salvage. My brain got the brunt of it, and now, in vengeance, it's connecting wires like a mad scientist might, trying to build the atom bomb, working up the nerve to let loose and go wild. But then I grab something; a memory, a breeze, and I'm back! Back to the living world. Back to sanity. It's enough of an edge to keep me going.

I used to like him—Dali, the painter—but now I'm living a painting! The *Dali* world has become a nightmare.

It started with dreams. 'Nightmares' they're called. Only I wasn't dreaming—I thought I was. I thought I was about to wake up; that any second I'd be sitting in bed, calling for water, a comforting hug, a reassurance, an escape. But I never woke up, and this dream—this other—has been going on for years so I can almost laugh about it. But mostly in the dark, I want to cry.

A few birds like kites float above the expanse. They're tethered to strings as they hover in circles. This isn't normal, I know, but bear with me. It's what I see. The world's in motion and I'm standing still, an onlooker, a witness to the wonder of chaos. Shadows of grey and black stretch around me. There's a sound buzzing—a voice, a whisper. What do they want now? What should I say? Am I supposed to be grateful? Glad for the show? When other people see what's there? And I see this? That's what makes it so *awful*. So *fucking awful-I-can't-bear-it*. Not what I see, but that the majority don't! They see something different. They have the consensus so they're correct. I'm the one at fault; I'm the one immoral enough that I had to alter reality. Maybe they're mad and I'm sane but I doubt it. I scratched that idea away long ago.

A scientist is ostracized when he's ahead of the curve, and this is something I've believed to be a pattern. He gets cast out because he knows better. Because he's smarter. Because he's just and honest and a swell dandy guy. Only I don't know better, I know worse. I'm not ahead of the curve, I'm off the *fucking wagon*. I'm wandering the desert far gone from the road!

I lean over some tulips which grow splayed through the tillage. There's a flowerbed lining the sidewalk which stretches up to the building then continues around front then along the side—sneaky and somnolent—like the whole thing was a moat with waters so dark they would swallow me up if I ventured in. First the limbs, then my mouth and nose, until eventually I'd choke and die. But none of this would occur before I started yelling like a madman. I could imagine myself screaming, desperately trying to get out of the moat. And then, upon running from the hospital door to rescue poor Zhukov, would they only find a young man rolling around in the dirt? I doubt it, but it seems likely. This seems to be the general pattern with me.

When I got here this morning the building had a sun-star reflected on the black windows like the institution was a company that worked in computers. It's a hospital but you'd think it was a tech firm. The plaque was there with the founders' names, like they are meant to last. Names engraved so deeply they're under my skin. The trees surrounding the hospital were swirling and the lawn was complaining about the lawn mower again and the man who operates it. But it's these flowers I like best and these I see now. I smell the scent up into my brain. What a wonderful smell. To smell tulips is like poetry, each conveying its own coded message and its own sound. I pull back from a petal as it stings my finger. I nearly swear.

Boy, that hurt!

A little bee flies off and disappears in the sky, then I see it hovering up near the glass and a moment later it's gone from sight. I stand there, looking at my wounded finger, holding it up, eyes squinted in the sun. But it must have been *that* kind, I think. The kind which doesn't lose the stinger.

"Thanks," I say, voice laden with sarcasm. But I don't begrudge. Not really. It's pretty natural to sting when you're afraid. But I suppose I just feel…I don't know…hurt.

But the locution of speaking is what I'm talking about now as I hone back in on the flowers, refocusing. My concentration has to be perfect. This is its own art and craft and it doesn't come easy. Speaking to flowers is a fragile matter mostly because they're as stand-offish as cats, or as talkative as gossips—those women over hedgerows who yammer on and on. But they (the flowers) talk and are silent. They whisper and yell. When I talk to tulips I never know which. Will they talk today? Will they rave like lunatics? Will they whisper in hushed tones? Will they ignore me?

It began when I was younger at the age of 3 in a small town outside Leningrad. That's where I got some training in being crazy and took my first steps into madness.

That's what I want to talk about, here. That I want to be like most people. But while others see plants—green plants or flowers, it doesn't matter—I'm seeing a spectrum. A symphony of colours like a rainbow. I hear what they say. When others watch birds I am smelling what they've eaten. I'm touching their wings. I can feel feathers.

The teachers at the school thought me odd. 'We all know there's something wrong with that boy, but what's he doing in school? He should be in one of those facilities, shouldn't he?' I had made friends in school despite my difference, but the teachers had always eyed me that way, like they didn't trust me, as if I might pick up the ruler at the chalk-board and beat them to death with it. I could almost laugh at those looks of fear. And the humour went further than some of them know. Oh, how far it went! I played along, to amuse myself with the foolish fears, especially, and most frequently, of middle-aged white women, who believed, for some reason, that others wanted to rape them, or maybe just kill them. And all the while, they seemed afraid of me! Me! Why, I don't know. But the ego of these women so scared of black men and crazy people, too. When it's black men, they're dressed in a suit and tie—clearly businessmen with no criminal intention, clearly with no intention to harm. With crazy people it's anyone who acts crazy enough to give them the impression they're actually nuts. They've seen too many movies. They've read too many crime novels. And that is what it's like to be crazy. It's like being a black man and it makes you appreciate what it's like to be him. The same scared looks, the same fast walking, the whispers and stares, the car doors locking. How ridiculous! And I would look at sharp objects, and stare like it amused me. I would stare until the adult grew so nervous they withdrew. If they only knew how much I was laughing! Laughing my 12-year-old ass off. Laughing because it made me feel better. It made me feel sane. It made me feel like I wasn't the one being pointed out. Like no one was looking at me as odd in this big game of fear and misunderstanding. I had no desire to harm any person. I didn't even kill flies! But I knew how they felt, and got a laugh from their fear. Scaring them silly with their own petty ignorance.

There are few jokes greater, only a handful so just.

But when I came to the hospital, Doctor Parkston was different. I remember him in his silk tie, shined shoes, and stiff collar, stepping out of his BMW into the African dust. I stood on the sidewalk smoking a cigarette as I admired the monkeys. The man walked up to me with a confident stride. His shadow seemed to fall over me and block out the sun. Through the sun haze I could see a big toothy grin. He stuck his hand out without hesitation, then he showed me around and put his hand on my shoulder and acted without fear towards my insanity and showed no regret for hiring me; even when he discovered my insanity may be worse than first expected from our talks on the phone. Parkston was on a mission. It didn't seem to matter if you were crazy or not, because he accepted you. He made you feel like you belonged. I'm sure a lot of people could relate to this. Everyone's known someone who made them feel welcome. Made them feel like they belonged, and possibly, even, that they were normal.

Even though the man himself is an oddity, I can almost like him as a father figure. But at once, in that wanting to admire him, I've felt an uneasiness, as if I couldn't quite do it. Perhaps this is the way others felt about me. And if that's so, then I'm sorry. But with me, it was ignorance. With him, it's something else.

I'm 21 now and still furtive about it. Still sweaty palmed and paranoid. Still worried they might come and take me away. Maybe the doctors, maybe men in black coats. I don't know and it doesn't bother me which. Let them come, I think. I'll be waiting. I've got a whole speech to give 'em when they come. I've got a laundry list of complaints and the first one is, *Why?* The second: *Why me?*

I'm looking behind me to make sure it's private but the monkeys have never ratted me out. I've got a few things I want to say before work.

What are you? I ask.

I'm a tulip.

I know that.

Then you know all there is to know.

I'm trying to get a conversation going, but they're silent as snow, as silent as the day I first walked past in what seems like ages ago. It was the month of June, a little warmer than now, but then, it's warm in Cameroon. We're directly on the equator so I'm sweating my balls off.

I walk through the doors and hear the air conditioner blowing like wind through a mountain pass. I've been walking through this door all my life. This front door was the birth canal I must have slid out of. It's like being reborn after a safe night in the womb. I enter each day to find I don't understand. That I don't understand the world I've come into.

To my left is the staff lounge where people drink coffee. They're in there now, chattering like maniacs, starting off the day with a bang. I can hear 'em yammering, on and on, like they're afraid of the silence, insecure in some way. Like laughing would chase away the fear looming over them. In front of me is the hall which leads to the action. But to the left? To the left are the maniacs.

I'm standing in the cool. I'm wallowing under shade like a new born calf! I'm in the middle of two worlds, powerless. Mostly I'm powerless to make one real. It's dark and I can hear sounds moving, breaking rhythms of breath, whispering secrets. It's like faded photographs telling me a history. But

I'm still standing stiff as a board. *I've got to wait for it to start,* I think. *If I don't wait then there's no telling if it started or if I took off without it.*

Then there's that sound of a phone ringing, an audible voice like a lilting laugh. It's started, I decide. Then I'm moving like ice, smelling lemon cleanser, kicking up dust left by so many feet. They were feet in faded procession. Large feet and small feet, and feet barely feeling; feet with legs which were partially crippled, then wheels for those who couldn't walk. What is a hospital, but a sponge which absorbs? Absorbs the bacteria—the human sicknesses—but not the humans. The people walk out but the sickness remains. It's heaped and heaped until the whole place is scrubbed. And boy, do they scrub it! You should see the janitor with his mop bucket and mop, scrubbing floors after a long day of use. Scrubbing hard while bacteria grow. Scraping away at the layer of refuse. I can see him down there, mopping in rhythm; a rhythm which doesn't change a thing. It only delays the inevitable, I think. But he doesn't seem to know it. That the hospital is eventually going to get sick. The hospital is eventually—if it hasn't already—going to crumble to the earth and let out a heave before it all comes down in a scattering of wreckage.

A patient groans from a room as I pass, then I bump into a doctor as he swings around the bend.

"Oh there you are Zhukov."

Zhukov! Zhukov! Zhukov, all day long. I hear my name but I barely understand it!

His face looks yellowish like wet dandelions, black eyes glimmering behind coke bottle glasses, white coat sweeping to the floor. When he speaks, it's like ice on my spine; a certain locution which causes unease.

"I was wondering," he says. "If you wouldn't mind checking up on our anonymous patient. She has a fever."

"I can do that."

"Good," he says firmly, then sucks up a big breath. "That will make my day a lot easier." Then he sweeps down the hall like a transient flower—if that could be it—colours fading around him as he moves into darkness. The gloom seems to follow him wherever he goes. I've wondered, but never found the answer to that. I follow him with my eyes as he turns at the bend. I think, *He's going to do scary stuff too. Stuff which would scare yeh just to watch it.*

I continue on until I get to the big room. This room is like a basketball court, or something. Like those basketball courts I've seen on TV, but the wrong colour and the wrong smell; a large rectangle we call the ICU where we stack all the patients who are sicker than others. I walk down the rows and it's an ugly sight. I stop in my tracks. My head's holding me back so I can't figure it out. Which way I'm going, and all. Wait now! Walk! Wait now! Walk! I'm going out of my freaking mind. I have to count backwards to find the harmony and find the note. I have to before I can set things right. When I do that, I can continue on. It's an odd hesitation of the brain, causing motor functions to fail, causing worlds to unravel and lights to flicker and wind to rush. I'm looking at the woman on the bed before me. I've got her dead in my sights like a sniper on a rooftop, and I realize, this is the woman. This is the woman I'm supposed to be treating.

Her legs are splayed and her arms are bellicose, like she had been run over by a melon-truck, or something. Right down the middle. It's moonstruck to look at. You can almost see the tread marks, like whatever had run her over, kept going, like I had to squint to make things real. But the tread marks are there: two black lines from the front and back wheel, right up her face then onto the wall, straight up to the roof where they keep going. I think, Maybe she's a machine come undone at the bolts, left on the table to collect dust. And boy, I start getting angry. Not so angry I'll explode. But I'm angry at whoever left her like this. I'm angry 'cause it's really despicable. I place my satchel on the night-stand and pause to think. I close the curtain, then I pull out the thermometer and lay it down flat to think about things. It's pretty messed up to look at her. I stand up then lean over her and start going to work. I'm doing a procedure which has rules to adhere to; an honourable craft to make her look more presentable. I move an arm, then leg, twist a hand, and presto! I lay things just so like a body in a coffin.

Once done, I stand back and take a look at my work. I do it like a builder might look over a fence to analyze the work he's done and see if it's correct. Straight as a string, I think. I feel proud. But it can't last. To look at her, it would make some sick. I stick the thermometer in and start dissecting the psychology, trying to figure out what's bugging me so much. She really looks sick. Sick to think of. Sick to remember. I should run away and get one of the masks. But I'm fine, I think. I hardly ever get sick from what they've got here, and she's not even coughing. She's really asleep. If they're coughing that's different, but if they're breathing, I'm fine.

I'm ready to pull the thermometer out in case she wakes up and bites down. This can be an issue of paranoia and fear, but rarely a reality. Still, it would be a disaster. Mercury poisoning isn't high on my list of mistakes I'd like to make today.

I pull the thermometer out and take a look. The line reads 103. That's pretty bad. If it gets much worse, well…let's hope it doesn't. I replace the thermometer then pick up my satchel and start down the room again, walking quickly. I've got patients to see and not a lot of time.

"Zhukov!"

It's the head nurse and she's in a real bind. She comes walking up in a fluster, bees buzzing around her head and eyelids fluttering like hummingbird wings.

"Zhukov." She seems exasperated. "I was wondering if you could go to room 109. I have another fever there."

"I can do that."

And I don't mind doing it for her. She's a pretty nice gal. She always asks and never orders. Even though I work under her, she's always polite.

"Thanks," she says, then sweeps off in her dress. She's the only nurse who'll still wear a dress to work.

"Zhukov, you've got to go see the doctor today."

Nooooo. No. No. I don't want to! ANYTHING BUT THAT! ANYTHING!!!

But she's standing there with her hands on her hips. She doesn't understand what it's doing to me. She doesn't understand what it can do to a little boy. To have him examined. To have him prodded with thermometers. To have him analyzed and interrogated, and made to feel small. I'm already small. I've got a slight limp from when I jumped over the fence and tried to run down the street in the middle of winter. Only four years old and I managed to climb a fucking fence! Imagine that! Imagine a little boy so desperate to get away that he had to climb over fences. He's four years old and already running from the law.

But my mother stands there with her hands on her hips, then she leans down and kisses me on the forehead. Like that's going to make it all better!? A kiss on the forehead? Really, mom? But it helps a little, let me tell you. If she could only see that it helps to show affection then maybe she could see that it would help even more…if I didn't have to go to that place!

Whyyyyy? Why do these women have to trust men with D.R.? Doctor. I hear doctor this, and doctor that. He's just a man with a piece of paper! Psychology is a pagan religion. But they've got D.R. in front of their names. Might as well be high priest of the Aztecs. Why do they trust them more than the little boy who is crying out?

She finds me under my bed, and I'm crying.

"Zhukov…Zhukov honey…"

I DON'T WANT TO GO.

Doesn't she get it?

I'm holding a thermometer just like the doctors who screwed me up. Here I am walking the hallway. Here I am, screaming to be left in peace and all the while I'm doing the same fucked-up things; the same implacable things they did! I look into the patient's room where it's dark like a cave. A wind blows through and scares me inside and here I am listening for the sound of the wind and hoping this wind won't find me in here. I can see the tall guy on the bed; a silhouette in darkness; a man shape. I hear him snoring like slumberous creatures huddled together in a cave. I catch myself walking to the blinds, pulling them wide so I can see what I'm doing. The sunlight breaks through the wall, and SMASH! Like a wrecking ball that touches my skin, crawls up my back and warms my face like a hot towel. I walk to his bed and grab the visitor's chair, then I pull up close and sit. It's almost awkward being so close. He wakes up as he's sensed me, sees me with his x-ray vision, knows I'm just scared about the whole thing. So now he and I are in this together.

"I have to take your temperature," I tell him, placating and polite.

He doesn't nod. The guy watches me and we start our allemande. I take a thermometer and stick it in his mouth but he spits it out. It nearly falls on the floor! I suck in a scared breath as my hand darts out. I catch it just shy of the edge.

"Why…" I start to say. But it's no use, I think. "I need you to keep it in your mouth." I sort of stick my finger in my mouth and keep it there. I think maybe this is the way to explain it.

I stick the thermometer in and he keeps it. We wait. We almost hold hands, waiting for the outcome. Waiting for the little red line to drop.

I can see he's got a fever as I remove the glass tube. He's kind of shaking as people do when they're overheated and really cold.

"What's your name?" he asks me, weakly, strained.

"Zhukov."

"Shu-cov."

"You have a fever," I say. "The nurse took most of your blankets so that you'd cool down."

I can see he's shivering, too. Boy, that must be a pretty bad fever.

"It's your core body temperature. That's why you feel cold. You're trying to cool down and your core temperature has dropped."

The jungle engulfs me on both sides. Then, on one side, is a veldt filled with cookfires, and shanty homes which have been assembled from spare parts. Onwards and outwards towards a hazy horizon are birds, I think. Hate-filled birds, masked and mangled, ready to spread their wings and start over the grasslands, no doubt in search of something dead. *Change, Change, Change, before we go down with the dust,* I think. When I come around the bend I'm presented with a hospital; tinted windows gleaming with sun-stars. The grass and building have been dropped on top. Really wedged in there like the shovel's first slice. I'm not sure, but I think that beneath that grass there are growing things and animal things. Some of them waiting to get free. They are waiting to break through the grass and start spreading, moving in a mangled mesh of life, which will take the hospital; which will eat it *whole.* I can almost hear them moving.

That's how the day started: with pseudo philosophy. It started with a reflection of my subconscious.

She's moved. Her legs are parallel and her hands are folded like a corpse in a casket. But she's not dead. At least, *I hope she isn't.* Her whole demeanour seems calm and pleasant. The perspiration is gone from her brow, swept away by the air conditioner.

I put a soft hand on her forehead. I want to get a reading. She feels cooler to the touch—far from what I expected when I first saw her lying here, sweating through the sheets, and barely conscious. I reach in my satchel and pull out a thermometer. The thermometer is the sword of the medical staffer. I make a note for her chart, but it's just an opinion. Hands won't cut it when it comes to the chart. I need to use the thermometer because it's the only way. If I do that, I think that the temperature will drop.

I slip the thermometer under her tongue like I'm doing something obscene. Preliminary rape is what this feels like. She opens her eyes and I jump back. She scared me pretty bad. I must be sweating, she scared me so bad. As we exchange looks, I mumble something apologetic. It must be like an awkward crossroads. I feel I've been caught with my hand in the cookie jar. Boy, is it awkward. I want to shrink up and slip off. But it's just her and me and I've got to stay. I have to make sure she's better.

My eyes are wandering around the room. I mean, maybe it's more awkward for me, 'cause I was the one trying to pull a fast one.

I nod to her. She seems to nod back. She doesn't fight my advance, so I move in again. I re-adjust the tube where it's hanging down like a cigar. When I pull it out, I can see it's gone down.

I sigh.

"Pardon, Miss. What's your name?" I ask. Maybe I can get a conversation in after all.

She stares at me then moves her lips. It's like the sound is trapped inside some well. When she speaks, I nod. I don't speak a word of the Swahili she's speaking. I learned French from growing up in Quebec, and a little more here at the hospital. But we've got over 200 languages here. Still, I want her to feel that she can talk to someone, so I act as if I understood.

"Parlez-vous français?"

She shakes her head no.

"Parlez-vous anglais?"

No again.

The head nurse sweeps by and sees us talking.

"Oh my, is she doing better Zhukov?" *Voice full of cheer.*

"I suppose."

"I'll get the doctor."

Then sweeps off like a broom, her dress swishing.

"Comment ça va?" I ask.

"Ça va."

I smile. Good. She's feeling fine and she speaks a little French.

"Bien?"

She shrugs.

"Ça va."

Yes, I think. *Ça va* seems it. It won't be *Bien* yet. Not for a little while at least.

I hear soft shoes on the floor. They're the shining shoes of the doctor, I think. He's got those shoes shining and polished so that I think he must sit in his office for hours, shining shoes while the patients sleep. I turn around and see he's got his clipboard handy. Man can never be too far from that. Not in a hospital, no siree.

He takes his stance at the end of the bed like he's sizing her up against the length of his shadow, to see who's bigger, and all.

"Bonjour."

I explain to him that she doesn't speak French. He frowns deeply and accentuates his wrinkles. It's pretty hilarious, but I try not to laugh.

"That's too bad," he says.

"She speaks Swahili."

I wonder now if my days carrying around a thesaurus have helped me with languages. I use quite a few esoteric words, but then I'm pretty normal besides that.

Dr. Parkston ignores me and looks around. It seems he's fixing something up. I can always tell when doctors are fixing something up. He's got that same worried look and he's looking around. I'm not sure why there would be any concern. I've never seen him do anything illegal. He moves the clipboard to his side. It's suddenly in the way, apparently. Then he looks up to the wall above her.

"She has AIDS," he says to no one in particular.

"Mmhmm."

"The antibiotics have fought off her flu but she could get sick again."

I knew that too.

"I'm going to administer a new drug called Nevidil."

A new drug? I think about that. They're always trying new drugs. That's part of what this hospital does.

He pulls a bottle of pills from his pocket and I can't figure out why he already had them. He flips up the cap with his thumb, then tips the bottle over and spills two pills out. He seems to examine them carefully. He's moving his hand up and down to weigh each pill in his mind. He hands them to the woman and she takes them. Her hands are trembling but there's no hint of concern. She doesn't seem the least bit worried. She pops 'em in her mouth, then dry swallows and lets on a smile which says 'All done'.

Dr. Parkston takes in a big suck of wind. My imagination must be tricking me.

"Good. Good. I'll be back to check on her personally." He looks at me with steady eyes. "You don't have to worry about her anymore Mr. Zhukov. Just check on your regular patients. I'll worry about Miss…"

"She never said her name," I say cheerfully.

He just waves his hand dismissively.

"Well. I'll worry about her," he says.

I'm standing in a black suit. There is no one here but friends from my mother's work. We left most of our family behind in Russia. So here I am standing over my mother's grave while a minister reads from the Bible. I don't know why I can't cry. I suppose a lot of people have that problem. They just can't cry when they know they should. But it's really bothering me and I'm trying to make myself sad. I'm thinking of all the stuff that we've been through and that's when it hits me and I just break down. But I'm crying too much now. The minister is sort of looking at me out of the corner of his eye. That's when I just let it go and I curl up in a ball on the grass. I'm just dying here. I'm crying for it all. I'm crying for my childhood. I'm crying for my mother. I'm crying for Julia Gardner behind the dumpster. I'm crying for Jimmy Canelop who tried to get some people to beat me up after school the next day. I'm really dying here and some people have to take me away after that. I end up back in the mental hospital and it's not for another month that I'm let go. All I can think of is the shocked look on all those faces when they dragged me away.

My mother's dead here!!! Can't a guy cry a little?

"CLEAR!"

The paddles shock her. She convulses like a mannequin moving in one piece. It's disturbing.

"What's going on?"

"CLEAR!"

Again. Same reaction. She's diiiieeing.

Again she convulses. Finally the doctor wipes his forehead and calls the time of death. What happened?

The doctors and nurses clear out like they all had places to be, like they're scattering from a foul stench. The woman is still here! I'm the only one left standing like a tree in a field or a man holding his hat in his hand over some grave on a Sunday. She was doing just fine. Just peachy keen. I keep repeating it over and over in my mind, trying to figure out what they were saying. It was something about a 'side-effect' to the 'drug'. 'Pulmonary-something'. 'Cardiac'—'BP over 200'. What did these phrases mean?

I walk over to the bed, put both hands on her shoulders then shake her gently to see if she'll stir. She doesn't move. She's definitely dead. A nurse comes back and I can hear her sneakers. She's sneaking up behind me, but I won't leave the woman. This nurse speaks like she's soothing a child.

"Zhukov. I'm sorry. We're going to have to move her now."

"Fine," I say bitterly. I stand up straight and take a few steps back.

The orderlies are coming now. I can hear their wheels squeaking. They wear blue scrubs but they don't heal anyone. They only take the dead away and push the crippled around. They slide a stretcher up to the bed. I see one of them has a nametag on. I'm expecting him to ask if he can take my order. They lift her onto the stretcher and place her on the bag. It's a black bag, the colour of death. I'm watching the whole thing and looking around. I'm looking to see if many patients have noticed. I look back to watch them as they go to work. They wrap the top up, then they zip it up so she's encased in that blackness. I watch them wheel her through the back exit. First they'll use the elevator to get downstairs. It's the difference between life and death in this place. Either floor 1, or the basement. You're either living or in a freezer or up here. There's a short trip in between to mark your passage. The whole thing is like a funeral procession.

Dead, I think. Just like that.

I rub my fingers together then start looking around.

I look for the answer and know it in my mind. It was that drug; she'd be alive if not for that stupid drug! I start getting angry like a firecracker going off. It's just flying around causing all kinds of trouble. I see the firecracker hit the wall then soar across the room and break through the window. I don't even know why, but I better calm down. People can loose tempers and jobs. That is if they don't calm down. I think I want to punch something. When I get angry like this—and it barely ever happens—I just need to take a breath.

I do. I breathe in a breath of that hospital air. I take another one. It feels better.

I start calming down. I can feel the room coming back to me.

I've got to keep going 'cause I can't bring her back. Not just by being angry, I can't. *Or can I?* I wonder. I'll add that to the list.

I hear that groan again and stop in my tracks, listening for sound, holding my breath. I walk back a short distance then look around. It's silent but for the normal sounds of the hospital. I can hear a phone ringing as I look up at the numbers. I try to think. The sound had come from room 113.

No wonder, I think, *'cause 13's an unlucky number.* This hospital must have been built on the 13th. Built in some cold month in hell. If you build the whole thing on an unlucky day, that's the end of it, let me tell you. I can picture them doing it. *They've got a big crane and they're swinging a steel frame into place and there's this crooked looking man in a plastic helmet with a cigar in his mouth and he's ordering the workers to work faster 'cause they've got to finish the whole thing on the 13th or else the curse won't work! So he keeps snapping his whip at their backs to make 'em work fast, and by God, they're working so fast. They've got to finish this place before the day is out! And in the end, when all the dust is settled and the sun is going down a reddish hue, the whole place stands in blackened glimmers. They completed the whole darn horrible thing and the foreman with the cigar is just smiling like a manic devil because he's so pleased they got it done. Now women and children can come here to die, he thinks. And if the hospital itself doesn't get 'em first, dumbass drugs with stupid names will do the trick alright!*

I hear that groan again and I open the door a crack. It's like I'm sneaking around. There's a tall, old black guy lying flat on the bed and his feet are almost hanging off the end. They really should have longer beds in this place. Most of the beds are imported from Europe where people are shorter. I can see the old guy isn't happy about it either. He's sweated clean through the sheets and there's a big frown on his face.

He looks up with hollow eyes then says something in dry French like there's cotton balls on his tongue.

"My mouth is dry."

"Would you like some water?" I ask.

"Merci."

I go quickly to the room's bathroom. They've got these bathrooms just right to of the door, but most patients are too sick to use them. I take down a paper cup from the ledge. Then I pause. I take down another cup and fill 'em both 'til they're almost over-flowing with that crisp clean water. I've got to spill a little out or I won't be able to carry them both. I walk into the room and see he's just licking his lips. You can tell he hasn't been taken care of, and he's just dying to have some of that cool clean water that tastes so good when you're thirsty like that.

I hold the cups out for him.

The man reaches up with shaking hands and grips a cup like it's a golden grail. He tilts it back and spills a little down his chin. He's drinking so fast, and he's so thirsty.

"Good. Yes. Thank you, young lad."

He licks his lips like a jungle cat.

I offer a second cup and he drinks like before. When he's done, he leans back and let out a sigh, then he looks at me really appreciative-like.

"What's your name?" he asks.

"They call me Zhukov."

"Zhukov. Where did you get that name?"

I think about it.

"My mother was Russian. We moved to Canada to escape the bad men as we called them."

"The bad men? Yes, I can see what you're talking about. But what did they want with you?"

"They thought I was crazy." I shrug. "They weren't nice about it. That's all I really remember."

And *that's* really the fact of the matter.

The man looks at me with understanding then nods and closes his eyes. I can tell when people are tired. That's something being on the ward will teach you: when people are tired. I think he's passed out and that's well and fine. *Just peachy keen.* He needs his sleep because he's sick with the flu. I step out of the room, then start down the hall—to see if I can find someone to talk to.

Doctor Parkston: *We have a responsibility to make progress.*

Myself: *I was just wondering what happened is all.*

He looks at me with black glimmering eyes. He wears glasses so you can see them glimmer by sun pouring through his window. I've been here 20 seconds and I already don't like it. It's kind of stuffy and you can really see particles floating around. I can't stand that. I have real issues with dust. I've got mild allergies and I want to sneeze, but I'm holding it in to be polite. The doctor's sitting on the other side of his desk just watching me from time to time. He's got one hand and arm on the desk and he seems uncomfortable, but you can tell he's doing his best to act fine. He always seems to indulge me, and I wonder if that's because he feels bad about what happened. Maybe he wants to talk to someone, I think. I would. But if you want to know, something about him gives me the creeps.

He has a way of looking at you as if he might start throwing stuff.

"...it's a bit of a conundrum," he's saying now. Boy, is he ever getting into the lecture. "The Helsinki Declaration forbids human experimentation. But what are we to do? We can test the drugs out on lab rats, dogs, cats, even lions. But eventually a human has to try it first. We don't know how it will react in humans until we take that step. Someone has to try the drugs first..."

I'm starting to get bored. I'm really fading the way I can sometimes, and don't like him saying 'lab rats' and *her* together. But still, I can see where he's coming from. It's just, I mean, it's easy to look at it objectively when it's not someone you love or care about. But if she was my mother, I'd be pretty upset. Heck, I'm already upset. Upset and I didn't even know her name! I feel kind of pathetic, if you want to know.

"The Geneva Convention has been amended to allow drug testing when consent is given. The Nuremberg Code initially only allowed testing when consent was given directly by the patient. Now a legal guardian can give consent as well..."

He's really droning on now like an old broken record. He's looking off and getting into lecture mode, like he's trying to convince himself, or talk himself out of something. But he's only talking to himself...not *me*. I'm getting bored. I used to really like history. I used to read books about Western history. But I don't like hearing it at times like this. Nothing he's telling me is really helping. It seems to only be making it worse. He's just droning, and I can hardly stand it. My feet start fidgeting and then my hands.

PART II:
INDECISION

I come to two doors and step into the cold. What brought me down was in my head, but it's my feet which won't move now as if laden with iron. It's a little brighter than the hallway was. Rows of drawers glisten, like they're on parade. I can see my reflection as a vague, blurry image of colours and haze, and a blotch of paint and an ambiguity where bottles of disinfectant are stacked on a shelf. I look over and see a mop resting in the corner, damp and oozing. Beside the mop is a gnarled mop bucket which appears to have seen better days.

It smells like lemon and a sharp sting of cleanser. I don't like that smell suddenly and I don't know why. I take a quick scan. Something about the smell is too brutal. I'd be more comfortable with something softer. Something like apples or pine trees or earth. Even the smell of flowers would be nice. But lemon? Or this…this other smell. I shake my head. It's not supposed to be, I think.

The room's pretty big and I can see they've tucked her in, then placed her in a drawer and removed the stretcher for the next poor guy to take the trip down. I look and see a body bag and I pause a moment, staring at that thing like I could make it vanish. I think if I blink enough times it will. It's crumpled in the corner and seems obscure, but it's a body bag alright. I wonder if it belonged to her and it's like a punch in the gut or staring into a Barathrum or performing a cancrizans—like walking backwards in circles. I'm immediately appalled by the sight I'm seeing. I'm blinking repeatedly to make it disappear. The bag is a picture of death and its cruelty, a brief expression like a painting or poem, or picture for the newspaper with no need for an article. 'This is what we think of the dead', 'This is how we put them aside'. *No*, I think. *They don't take those body bags off until they take them away. Away to bury them.* But it's still quite a sight. If you saw it you'd think so. It's dirty and crumpled, and I know it's been used.

It's also quiet, like a tomb. And that seems fitting, considering the reality. I can hear the sounds of the air conditioning. I'm looking around, making sure I'm safe.

It's kind of surreal, but mostly dull.

There's a steel table where they perform autopsies, but it's deserted and menacing. The floor is concrete and there's this drain for blood. Dirt too, I suppose.

There's dirt on some dead.

I'm drinking my coffee and looking around. I'm trying to figure out what they do down here. I've never spent a moment to really figure it out. I bet some mysteries are way down here with that pseudo-philosophy they quote in the high schools. Stuff that matters, but it's too hard to grasp. It would have to be, because it's hard to grapple with the facts. That you're going to end up raptured or here in a drawer.

I can't stand it any longer. I walk to the wall and pull out a drawer. The guy laying there has a scar on his cheek, features emaciated to skin and bone. He looks asleep and peaceful in death. His arms are parallel, lips tightly wound, like someone had done the work of making Jake Doe presentable.

I actually feel good about the way he looks. I think we should all hope to look as peaceful as that.

I push the drawer back then look around for the next drawer. Boy, I'm nervous now, to tell the facts. I'm not supposed to be down here, and all. I can imagine someone just barging in. They would know for sure I wasn't supposed to be down here.

I walk to the next drawer, crossing my fingers. I pull it out and hold my breath. But it's fine because this attempt's a winner. I can see she's looking really cold, almost blue in the light. Her face looks gaunt and unnatural and she gives the impression of fake-ness.

"Listen," I say. "I'm sorry. I didn't know they were going to give you that drug and all."

She says nothing and her eyes remain closed. I'm almost expecting her to move. She's dead of course, but I think maybe the dead can still hear you. That is, if you're sincere.

"I didn't mean for this to happen," I say to her. "I mean, I knew the drug was experimental, but I didn't think it was going to kill you. It's just, Doctor Parkston had to do it. You had AIDS so there was a chance you could get sick again and die. Unless of course you had enough money for the antibiotics and everything. You'd probably *live* if you lived in a developed nation. Most people with AIDS live, when they live in Western nations. You probably don't care about that, I know. I just wanted to say I'm sorry.

"My mom died from getting sick you know. I should have told you about that. You would have probably liked my mother. She was really nice and all. Really understanding. Did you have any kids? I bet you did. You probably had family anyways. Everybody's got some family somewhere. Most of the family I cared about is in Heaven. If you see 'em don't feel nervous or anything. They're really nice and you can just go right up and talk to 'em. Just tell 'em that you know *me*."

I look into her face then I push the drawer back into the wall. I wipe a tear from my eye. Man, I feel really pathetic. I usually don't cry, but it's happened before. I walk out of the room and start back up that hallway until I come to the stairs. This whole hospital was supposed to be a gift. It was supposed to be for the people. Its main focus is really drug testing, but the hospital supposed to be turned over when it was over. The people who fund this place are really nice. They're really just trying to help. Everybody is trying to find a cure for AIDS. It's a nice concept, but it doesn't always sit well with me. I've said that before but I can't say it enough. It's hard to figure out.

So I climb those stairs, taking one step at a time. This hospital has a basement and one ground floor. They probably never knew how many people would need it, or didn't have enough funding for a skyscraper like they wanted. The ICU seems lacking without her. The head nurse seems sombre as she walks, checking on patients and writing in her notebook, all the while with her eyes averted from me. I barely notice her now, but I notice comforting aspects. I see she has a hang-dog face. In fact, people have seemed very furtive. Less talkative, less manic. Maybe this place is learning, I think. But I'm starting to think something's screwed up. Like something about *her* case was all wrong. Crooked. Conceited. But when I start thinking that I'm usually paranoid. It's hard to know when you're usually paranoid.

I walk down the hallway until I find the janitor. He's an older guy with grey hair, and he's pushing a mop.

I start talking with him and he seems to be listening with a bit of a stand-offish-ness, uncertain about me. I lie to him about getting into the nurses' station. I need to get some things for Doctor Parkston, I explain. He seems to be buying it, and I feel bad. Mr. Omji is really a swell guy, if you knew him. He's always nice and always friendly.

He hands me a key-ring of jingling keys, holding them up like they were special. I thank him then start quickly up the hallway, trying to stuff those keys down my pocket. When I look into the nurses' station, I don't see motion. But that can change. I place the key in the lock and slide the bolt out, then step inside. There are these two computers along this really long desk. On the other side are filing cabinets where the patients' records are kept. Most of them are in alphabetical order but I don't have much time. I've got to be fast. If anyone caught me I'd lose my job. I start under 'W'. I'm thinking of 'WOMAN', or something like that. I must be a real idiot, I think. I broke in here but don't know how to find her. I hear footsteps in the hall and suck in a breath. Tap...tap...tap. My heart is thumping. Voices in my head. Telling me to run. I hold my breath for what seems like an hour. The foot-steps go past and the nurse walks by, sweeping by to get somewhere fast. She doesn't look sideways to me standing there: the idiot with the guilt on his face.

I exhale, then start breathing normally again.

Man that was close, I think. I could lose my job. I thumb my way over to 'W'. There's a lot of names in 'W' but I don't find any for just 'WOMAN'. I close the cabinet and check the next one. I feel like a vise is gripping down on my tenders, and all the while, I'm expecting someone to break in and find me and start yelling like a madman. I'm looking under the X names and thinking, *They might have just filed her under 'X'. The X-File! X-Woman! X-tra X-travaganza!* I keep flipping through all these hard-to-pronounce names, and eventually I come to this mangy folder.

'Patient X'.

I slide the folder out then start reading through symptoms 'til I come to 'Patient Sex: M'. I almost groan. 'Cause 'M' stands for male. There was bound to be more than one anonymous patient. But I don't have time for them all. I'm sticking the folder back and giving up when I see a folder marked 'Patient X-Woman'.

Bingo!

I slide it out. It's not very thick, but I look inside. Boy, they've taken a Polaroid and more. I just take the folder and get the heck out. I know better than to stick around at this point. The door closes behind me with a faithful click. And now I'm not sure what I'm doing; not sure why I did that. I'm walking down the hall, feeling good now and proud, like a weight had been lifted, as if the tide had turned, and all those cliché positives, and such. The janitor is mopping to a steady rhythm. I approach him, thank him, then give him the keys. And he smiles and thanks me, too.

Some people are really polite like that. They'll do you a favour then thank you for it. I think we'd all be better off if we did that.

I'm smiling now, feeling a real high. I must be going nuts again.

I'm sitting on this crazy bench made of tree logs, and I can hear the birds singing in the trees. Bees buzz precariously around flowers, like pagan worshipers around an idol. I wipe at my face with the back of my hand. I can really taste the salt sweat on my lip. The sun is blazing down on the grounds, beating the dust into submission.

Somebody made this bench out of logs. They left the bumps and waves and everything.

I'm shifting in my seat, here! Man, is it uncomfortable.

As if things couldn't get worse, this monkey starts up, and boy, he's just really going at it. It's like someone had stolen his banana. For a second I think he's sounding the alarm. So the doctors and nurses will come bursting outside. I really just want that monkey to stop.

Then, when I think it can't get worse, he stops. I start breathing normally again.

There isn't much here, I notice. I flip the page. I don't know much about hospital procedure, but I know you have to have consent. Especially for experimental drugs. It has to be signed. And that's just the thing. There's no consent here. Just test results and test results, but nothing signed. Everything works here, except this.

No form and no name. Maybe Dr. Parkston has got the form in his office. Littered among others like an insult. Heck, his office was messy. He could have the Declaration of Independence! The Helsinki Declaration; all the signatures for the Nuremberg Code. All of them shuffled away, so he could look at 'em every time.

I put the folder on my lap then look out at the road. A jeep is bouncing up through the jungle. I can hear it switching gears and revving up, then it swings by in a flurry. The dust fans off in thick plumes which fall over the grounds.

*Maybe if…no, that's not it. But just maybe I should…*I'm really losing it. Boy, I can really start to lose it. If you want to know, I'm starting to think bizarre thoughts. I'm thinking of what I should do and I'm thinking maybe this was part of some plan. Not a conspiracy. If I thought that, it would be part of the sickness and I can't think all paranoid, but I can keep thinking I should do something. I could call the police. Hey! And say what? *Hey officer. I think we've got a patient with no name who didn't sign a consent form. Officer: And who are you?*

Myself: I'm a schizophrenic who works at the hospital. (Click... buzzzzz.) Yeh, that would work out real swell and dandy. Freaking Superman saves the day. Really raise a riot and bang on stuff.

But I stop. Maybe if I tried, she'd know how sorry I was and this would never happen.

NEVER HAPPEN AGAIN.

The idea seems appealing. More appealing than a cigarette might. More appealing than a cold bath on a hot day. A little way to turn back time. To reverse the death just a little. And who wouldn't want that?

Something flashes in my head, like a sort of daydream in fast motion: *A picture of a lighter held up under paper; a flask filled with kerosene thrown around; a flame sluicing a wall and a curtain catching fire.* I shake my head. It's too hard to tell what thoughts mean and my head is starting to mess up, let me tell you. The doctors say, I should call someone, or check myself in if this starts to happen. But I'm in the middle of Africa... miles from home.

Satirical. Illuminating. Star-crossed.

These were words which seemed to jump off the page as I looked down on the somnolent book. Jay Louis it was hard to concentrate on an esoteric book in the middle of summer vacation. Mr. Cross— and his name bore it all—was always handing out these bogus assignments during the summer. A real premeditated dick. We had heard stories that it was coming and now that we were in the eighth grade it had finally happened. I had been stuck with this piece of boring old fiction that had more dog-ears than...well...a lot of dogs. I guess I'm not that clever and that's something you should know about me right away. When it comes to metaphors my English teacher always gave me a bad mark. I'd like to think of a few metaphors for him. He's like an evil stepfather who got evicted and forced to teach eighth graders how to read and write. But then again, that's more a simile isn't it? We had just learned about similes and metaphors and thought we were all geniuses for knowing the difference. It was practically like learning the difference between right and wrong. And maybe, I have to think about it, I didn't really know the difference between right and wrong back then, but like a child my heart was in the right place. And maybe that's what makes children more virtuous than adults.

Anyways, enough with all that pseudo-philosophical fare. I stuffed the book under the bed, and headed out for the day. The summer was calling. When you're young you know that you're supposed to have fun before it's all over. That's something Mr. Cross obviously didn't understand. Teachers were always trying to over-cram their students with learning. They were taskmasters. And that's a half decent metaphor I think. I could always imagine if they had servants back in the old days they would be the cruel kind who would get their heads chopped off. I had been reading The Hobbit when I was supposed to be reading that other book, and boy let me tell you, that J.R.R. Tolkien really knew how to write 'em. Wizards and giant eagles and goblins and swords. That was the kind of thing they should be teaching you in school. How the hell were kids supposed to 'appreciate literature', as our teachers always talked about, if they didn't have the type of material they could relate to? I had been reading The Hobbit at the same time as Tommy Sanders had. We were both competing with one another to see who could finish the book first. I had had to stay up all night with a flashlight one night because Tommy had gone on a reading binge and made it way past Rivendell and the moonstone and all the way to Mirkwood and the giant spiders. I had made it up to the point where Bilbo meets Gollum and had passed out with the book in my arms. Luckily I had woken up halfway through the night and put the book back under the bed. I doubt my mom would mind if she found me reading it, but when you're young it almost seems more exciting if you think you're reading something you're not supposed to. That was the way I enjoyed The Hobbit even more. While Bilbo was discovering the world of Middle Earth and all its secrets, I was discovering the world of Middle Earth in secret. And I guess that made it a double secret in a way.

So I was walking down the street, feeling proud of myself because I had gotten to the part where Bilbo gets washed out of the Elves' palace in a barrel, thinking of how I was going to spoil it for Tommy, or show off how far I had read in the book, when I saw Julia Gardner riding down the street right before she looked away and slammed straight on into a car. I almost laughed out loud, but not really, because it looked like she might have really hurt herself. And I wasn't so mean as to laugh when someone was really hurt and all. I ran up to her and looked down. She was wearing a helmet, but she was trying to pull it off.

"Jay Louis," she said.

That was mmyyy word I thought. Nobody said that but me, and I thought for a moment maybe we had some sort of connection.

I put out my hand and she took it and I helped her to her feet. She brushed herself off but she didn't have a scratch on her. I still don't know how she managed that.

"Well this is terribly embarrassing," she said, as her voice took on a musical quality. "Absolutely un-lady like."

She talked funny for her age. That was one thing I noticed about her right off the bat.

"Do you need help walking home?" I asked, because for some reason, maybe it was the interested way she spoke, I was suddenly really interested in her; wanting to be around her and all that.

"What a gentleman," she said. "That would be delightful."

She reached down and picked up her bicycle. There was a dent in the car and some scratches, but neither of us seemed to think we should leave a note or do anything about it. We started walking down the street in the middle of summer. I knew her from school but I'd never talked to her. She lived down the road a few blocks and I thought I had seen her house before. It was the one with all the potted plants. Her mother must have been one heck of a fierce gardener and all.

"So you're John Zhukov," she said. "I've seen you play soccer. My little brother plays soccer and his games are always right after your games."

"Oh," I said. I wasn't sure I wanted her watching me playing soccer. I guess I thought I kind of stunk at playing. I was alright, but I wasn't a star athlete or anything even though I tried hard.

"Aren't you going to say something about me now?" she asked. "You know, ask me a question." She said it still with a musical and charming (that was the word for it, maybe witty and charming) quality to her voice. But she was pretty odd. Quite odd, as Mr. Cross might say when he was trying to sound smart, I thought.

"What do you mean?" I asked.

"Well, isn't that the way conversations are supposed to go? I ask something, then you ask something and we get to know one another."

I shrugged.

"Um...what kind of sports do you like?"

"Ballet," she said. "I've always wanted to be a dancer. I think dance is magical, don't you?"

"I like magic," I said. "But I've never thought of ballet like that."

"Haven't you?" She looked off whimsically. "I think it's absolutely stunning and gripping. Provocative and sublime."

She was using a lot of adult words. She must have read the paper a lot, I thought. But then again I had been using some adult words lately ever since I started to read the Rings trilogy.

"Yeh," is all I said. "Sublime."

She looked at me and she seemed to smile.

"Have you ever had a girlfriend, Zhukov?"

Now that was a funny question.

"Well. Sort of. I've kissed a girl, if that's what you're asking."

"Oh really," she said, looking at me with what might have passed for a lidless wink. "You do get around then, don't you?"

I didn't really know what she meant by that. I didn't travel around town very much. I only went down to the river and over to Tommy's house every once in a while.

"What was it like?" she asked whimsically. "To kiss a girl?"

"Well. It was alright. I mean it was just a peck on the lips."

"Oh," she said, sounding just a tad disappointed. "Well that's something still, isn't it? Pretty romantic still."

I had never thought of it as romantic. The girl had been Bethany Hill, and it had been a dare to kiss her. We had both been dared and so we just kissed each other in the play-ground. That had been 6th grade.

We reached the house with the potted plants. Boy, there were a lot of plants in that yard.

She stuck out her hand delicately like we were supposed to shake hands now. I shook her hand and it felt kind of awkward. I wasn't sure what I was feeling.

"Well, nice meeting you, John Zhukov."

Then she rolled her bike up the driveway and into the garage. I turned around and started walking home. I thought, as far as handshakes went, that was probably the best handshake I had ever had in my entire life. I wasn't sure if it was her or me that had made the handshake like that—but it must have been her. She was the one who was different in some way; not like the other girls at school.

Then I saw Tommy walking up the street towards my house and I realized right then and there that I wasn't going to spoil the book for him. Because something about that book—The Hobbit—just seemed a little bit…I don't know…sacred and pure to me. Not quite like religion but something I wanted to hold up in the light and then be careful with the pages. I never dog-eared any page in that book and I never will. Some books look better and it feels right. With others it just isn't supposed to be.

So Tommy Sanders strolls up to me and says, "What's up, you bastard?"

We had been swearing for the past 3 months. It was very cool to swear at that time.

"Nothing much," I said.

"You want to go to the river?"

I knew that Tommy wanted to go down to the river so we could jump off the bridge. But that was starting to get old for me. I don't know, maybe we had jumped off that bridge too many times. It was something which used to be awesome and now it seemed kind of lame.

"I don't know," I said. "You want to play blackjack instead?"

"Why not?"

We walked into the garage where we did most of our hanging out and I pulled the cards off the top of a tool chest. We used a cardboard box upside down to play. We brought the box out to the driveway and sat down there and I began to deal.

Tommy kept getting close to 20 and even got blackjack a few times. I was losing badly in our made-up sports score. We scored by hands. Whoever won the most hands won. We played to 15 hands. Tommy won quickly that time. It only took about 30 minutes for him to win, then we didn't have anything else to do again. Everything was so simple back then. Every decision a small one.

Parkston: "No, I'm afraid her consent form would be in her file, Zhukov. I can't let you into the nurses' station. Her information is confidential."

Myself: "I understand."

And I think, *Boy, do I understand. There isn't no fucking consent form and now we both know it.* Dr. Parkston is sort of scratching his head and looking off into the light in the ICU, eyes filled with light but giving back little warmth. The head nurse seems to overhear us and shoots a furtive look—really pursing her lips—then heads back to work where she's changing a bedding. There's this old guy just standing there watching her work. He's wearing a gown, waiting for the bed.

I feel bad for the guy.

Parkston walks off and that's the end of it. A back stiff and rigid and kind of insulting. He mentioned he's got places to be before he left. I watch him head out of the ICU, then I stroll around, just taking up space. I'm really kicking my shoes as I walk. Nobody is paying me any attention and that's just fine. *Just swell and dandy.* I'm really pissed now and my face must be twitching. I could really punch a big hole in the wall.

I'm thinking what I should do and I know I shouldn't be, but I can't help it. I think I once read this science fiction book, there was this character and they were talking about some plan. Overpopulation was this big issue, and people had to go, this guy was saying. Then this other character, he sort of pauses and says, "If we commit murder in the name of self-preservation, we will be good as dead inside and worse thereafter." And I'm running that over in my head how there's all these medical and experimental practices. I really don't know what to do, and I think, Heck, if I was a better person I'd know better than to just sit by. But they've infected me with their logic. I want to escape it and call it bad, and from the devil, and *fucked up*, but I can't escape what Dr. Parkston was saying. I mean, someone *does* have to try drugs first! They can't know what it's going to do until someone tries. But that's just fucked up, right? I mean, that's just screwy. You can't just experiment on humans, can you?

I shake my head and walk out the back door but I don't know where I'm going, though I'm walking fast. I start pacing up and down the hall, my fists in balls, clenching and unclenching.

I need to calm down.

I was 14 years old and standing outside the bar trying to get alcohol as we did from time to time. I had seven friends with me and we were hanging out. My mother asked, Where are you going? I said I was going out. I was going to hang out with my friends in the park. We were going to ride our bicycles around Laval. But then Jimmy got this bright idea like always. And eventually we decided to go to a bar. I really had been honest with my mother. I wasn't a big fan of going, of course, but then I wanted to keep my friends. If I'd known at the time it was going to be like this, I think I might have said 'forget it'. I might have just high-tailed it home, friends or no friends for my teenage years. But then we were hanging out around Misty's, and Jimmy gets this grand idea. He said it quietly like it was some great secret, about how he's going to get laid tonight. The other guys laugh but Jimmy seemed determined. I thought he might actually do it. When Jimmy set his mind to something he didn't let go. And I was thinking, I'm pretty lucky to have a friend like that. When Julia showed up, Jimmy takes her aside. He says he's got something to tell her. I watch them walk off into the darkness, and I'm actually wondering what the big secret is. Everybody leaves and it's just me again. Just me to be punished. Just me to intervene. I said I didn't want to go home quite yet. I said it because something told me this wasn't right. Something like a warning bell was going off in my head and I suppose even warning bells are right sometimes. Maybe I just knew Jimmy too well. Maybe I knew something about him he didn't. Something that made me worried. Worried that he might actually try something that night which would end any delusions I had about youth.

They're out back by the dumpsters where it's dark, and I'm in the side-alley, wasting time. I don't think Jimmy even knew I was there and I'm not sure I knew I was either. And that's when I heard a scream pierce the darkness. It was the scream I'd been waiting for but didn't want to hear. Somehow I knew the scream was coming. I didn't think I'd get away so easily. I crept up to the side of the alley. I did it slowly because I was unsure. I turned at the corner then peered through darkness. I didn't see Jimmy or Julia anywhere and for a moment I thought I was going crazy. But as I'm searching around I see where they are. Jimmy's on top of her and he's got a knife. He's holding it at her throat so she won't struggle, and she's lying still, almost paralyzed by fear. I can see a little blood where he's nicked her. She looks up past Jimmy, who doesn't see me. She's got terror in her eyes. Boy, that kind of thing really haunts me. I've woken up in the night to remember those eyes and somehow I feel they're part of me now. Like something of her got copied onto me. And when I look at the mirror I expect to see fear. At the time, I didn't know what was happening. I grabbed Jimmy and threw him to the ground. I wanted to do it before he could get up. I didn't think he'd use the knife on me, but I wasn't taking any chances.

"What gives, man?" He sees me now. He starts to get up but he can't find his knife. Finally he finds it and picks it up.

I tell him he'd better leave.

"I'm going to fucking stab you, man. Fuck you!"

I give a kick and he goes down again. Julia is up and she's running around the corner. Then I give another kick and this one breaks a rib.

I'm telling you, I've led a pretty strange life. But why does this stuff always happen to me? Why do I think that I'm probably violent? I get so worried that I run off. I didn't bother to look for Julia. I didn't stop running 'til I nearly collapsed.

There's got to be a solution, doesn't there? That's what every mathematician would tell you. Every evil can be expunged, can't it? You can always fire someone, send someone to prison. It's always someone's fault and never your own. It's usually someone with more power. This is the person people choose to blame: the government, the corporation, the ambiguous system.

I think about the ethics, and it isn't easy. But the consequences are those things we can't bear. And even I wouldn't want to and I'm as healthy as a horse.

The only correct thing would be to hold off on the testing. We should wait until they can figure it out. But then people would die! More people would die from not having drugs. And heck, we can always test appropriate candidates. People who are sure they're going to die. But…man, that just seems wrong, too.

I get to the staff lounge, which is deserted this time of day. Some of the staff keep cigarettes in here. I know 'cause that's where I used to keep mine.

I open up the cupboard above the microwave. I take down a pack and a lighter and think, they're not going to care. And I don't care either. I'd usually hate thievery, but I don't care now.

I'm heading out to have a cigarette and I might not come back. And I'm thinking, That's probably how tobacco was discovered. Some guy was trying to solve all these hard problems until he started lighting plants on fire. He was probably just as crazy as me.

I'm smoking by the road thinking through choices. *To be or not to be?* That wasn't a question. That was just laying out some options. What do you do when you can't do anything? Answer that one! As I'm thinking about it, this ambulance comes by. It's really calamitous and moving fast. Everybody's driving fast on this road.

That's something I noticed a while ago. I suppose they've all got places to be. I suppose the hospital is just another stop, and they don't really know what it's really about. That it's not just a point between A and B. That it's the last residence for some poor saps.

The ambulance is a transport vehicle of sorts. The name is different—a French phrase—but it's a transport for bodies. The thing comes to rest in a plume of dust and the driver kills the engine, then a spidery hand reaches out and flicks a cigarette away. I watch as it hits the dust in a fountain of sparks then lies burning. I'm listening to the sound of birds as I watch. They are singing it up, when these two guys hop out, bee-lining it for the hospital, hands in their pockets. I stroll over with my cigarette burning, smoke curling around me like incense around an idol. And I think, I must look really slick and all. And I'm not sure I like that. I'm trying to look casual.

"Can I get a ride into town?"

The taller guy stops in his tracks, looks me over with piercing eyes, as if he were wondering if I were actually for real. Then his mouth forms a deep frown and I know what he's thinking.

I explain I'm from the hospital. I try to make it sound like it's common. The expression softens.

"We've got to take one of the bodies away," he says in a hoarse voice.

"That's fine. I can wait."

The guy nods deeply then continues. He's got to hurry up to catch up with his partner.

I stand there smoking as they load a guy up. It takes 'em only two minutes to get him up to the grass. First they wheel him out really quick. They fly over the winding sidewalk, and I'm thinking, *Jay Louis! Take it easy!* They might just tip the stretcher and spill that poor guy all over the grass! But they don't seem to care much about what they're doing. They're really going at it, like it's a football game. When they get to the ambulance, they place the stretcher at the end and the other guy reaches under, releases this funny latch. He kicks up the wheels like an ironing board. They push the stretcher in then part ways, one heading for the driver's seat, the other taking it easy. It barely takes them 20 seconds.

I know they've got these coroners at this other place. The place in the city, which is better than here. And I know that he's going to the grave, one agonizing inch at a time. They take them to the city for the funeral arrangements, since most of the people live there, and want their loved ones close before they're moved to the grave. The bodies become like packages that get better treatment than a mailman would give. But that's what they've become. Packages.

Items.

We've all got to make money.

When they're finished with the stretcher, the guy at the back gets in without calling. I think the guy's hoping I forgot; hoping they could get away without taking me. I feel pretty bold. I want to stick my head in and laugh at him 'cause he thought he could get away. I walk over before he can close the door, then jump in with the body. I take a seat along this padded bench with these crazy tears. It looks like it had been through the French Revolution.

"You can't smoke in here," the shorter guy says, matter-of-factly.

No freaking kidding. I wouldn't have to if they weren't so quick to take off!

I toss my cigarette out and it hits the dust. I close the door with a chugging click. We're almost in pitch dark. Then the lights flicker. I'm in a techno bar. Like mood lighting, or something.

"What you doing in the city?" The guy checks the chart. He doesn't seem too interested as he does it; like he's performing a formality; he ferried people around all the time. He's got a short goatee and he looks at me—when I don't answer right away—wearily.

"I've got things I need to take care of," I say, then shrug. "I live there."

He nods, like it's all cool now. The driver puts the vehicle in gear, then we take off. I can really feel the bumps as we tear down that road. It doesn't seem to make sense. Like the guy was still alive and we were rushing him to surgery. I study the two guys in front of me. I don't know what to say. They're kind of the delivery boys of death. When I look at them I can tell they're professional about everything, but there's this carefree notion about their whole profession. It's more like they're trying to beat the clock.

We don't talk for the longest time. I didn't pay the ferry man or anything. I learned that in school, about the ferry man. When I die, I'm afraid I'll be too broke to die. I close my eyes, listening to tires. Nobody speaks. If the dead guy knew, he'd probably crack a joke.

I stroll into this little bar that has a green header and gold scrawl which reads: *Le depot de Liquor*. Pretty blunt name, if you ask me. But at least you know what you're getting. I came for alcohol. When I want a drink I'm pretty crafty about getting one.

When I walk in, the place is dark like a cave. There's smoke curling 'round the ceiling fans. They've got little round tables but nobody's in here except this guy passed out on a bar stool. The bartender is cleaning like it's important. He keeps his head down as he scrubs and he hasn't looked up at me once since I entered.

I slide onto a stool then ask for some beer.

The bartender starts at the tap. I don't know what I'm getting but it doesn't matter, I think. I'm pretty much looking for beer at this point.

A second later, a dark ale slides over. The guy throws the bar towel over his shoulder—like you see in movies—then walks over to check on the gangly guy. They guy next to me could be me in an hour. I don't want to watch him, because I've seen him before. I've seen him with my mind's eye and I've seen him in the mirror and I know what parts of his life are like. I'm feeling that way now, and I'm pretty sure I'll make it if I try. I look at the glass in front me. The glass is cool under my fingers. The CO_2 bubbles are floating to the surface, and I can imagine them going to my brain in a second. I can see them floating up to my head. I can feel them making me drowsy already. The beer's got a lot of head on it, I can see, like a pillar's been raised in my honour, or something. I know about alcohol. We've been acquainted. I'm looking at the glass to find the solution, but like every AA guy would probably tell you, it's just isn't there. But still, I'm studying the glass like it might be. Maybe if I could put it into words, I think. I keep staring at the glass and it comes to me: too much foam. But I'm cool with it and not the type to complain. I grab the beer and, *for crying out loud*, my hand's shaking. The guy must think I'm an alcoholic. I tip some back then take a big gulp. It goes down my throat feeling pretty strong, but not great.

Beer never tastes great when I'm out to get drunk.

The guy behind the counter's wearing a dress shirt and slacks. He looks professional with that really straight back. My back ain't so hot. I used to get back pain 'cause it was pretty messed up. But at least I never got on Oxycontin. That stuff will kill!

I'm watching the guy while he works. I'm just feeling angry for him now, outraged even.

He's a well-rounded black guy with neat spectacles, and he's apparently sporting the latest fashion, a goatee—really professional goatee, I think. If he looked more professional, he'd be on TV. He watches me to see if I'm satisfied, but I don't have the heart to tell him. So he looks back down then goes back to work. He's going to get that bar polished and clean.

"How long you been working here?" I ask. His lips are really pursed as he rubs. Then he looks up all of the sudden.

"Four years," he says with some pride. Then he puts both hands on the counter, almost beaming.

"You been in Cameroon long?"

"All my life."

He says it with some spring in his voice, too.

"What do you think of the Western World?" I ask him, really direct-like.

He looks me over, noticing my whiteness and Western accent, but I think he can tell I want a real answer.

"They're not bad," he says after a moment's thought. "They interfere in our politics sometimes and cause trouble. We tried to build a dam a few years back but these Western nature conservationists petitioned the government, claiming that it would endanger already endangered species." He shrugs. "So we never built the dam. We didn't want to endanger any animals."

I take a sip of my beer and notice it's starting to taste better. I'm feeling *vindication*.

"So you don't mind that people from outside your nation care less about your quality of life than they do animals?"

My tone is laden with sarcasm and distain. You can really hear it coming out laboriously.

He shakes his head and smiles, not sure about it.

"I'm not sure if it's like that. We had the choice to build the dam. We just didn't want to after it was over."

I nod. Seems fair enough. Perhaps I just wanted another answer. Something to really give myself a chance to rail at the Western World. I'm in a pretty bad mood, if you want to know, but the bartender is kind of killing my steam.

"They do a lot of charity work in the poorer areas," he continues. "A lot of people have the chance to grow up and get an education because of those Western Groups."

"Yeh," I said with some resignation. "A lot of good and some bad too."

He nods.

"Nobody's perfect."

Seems fair enough.

I say, "I think doctors are good people. And if they're not good people then what they're doing is good and that's got to rub off on the personality. It's a hard profession."

The guy's just staring at me. Probably wondering why I'm telling him this like he already kew I were a nut.

"...it's just, the decisions are so hard sometimes. Maybe that's what being a doctor is all about: being able to make the tough decisions even when you don't feel good about it. It's kind of like logic and reason over emotion. But sometimes compassion goes a long ways."

He just sort of nods to me like a simulacrum of my *superego*.

"...I work at this hospital you see. We treat these patients with AIDS. It's really an AIDS clinic. We're trying to find these cures and treatments but it's hard, you know? I don't know what to do. Sometimes I feel like...I don't know...like

I'm spinning into madness in that place. It's admirable but it's hard, yeh know? People like to complain but they haven't thought it all out. I don't know what to think."

I take another sip of my beer. I see I've almost finished it off.

"You want another beer?" the guy asks.

"Please."

He takes my glass and puts it under the tap then fills it up again and slides it over to me.

"...I don't know, man. I mean, bartenders are like psychiatrists right? I mean, they hand out advice and they hand out medication. Only their medication is alcohol. Every job is tough when you're dealing with human beings."

He nods. I think I've caught his attention. The guy at the end of the bar *groans*, lifts his head a little, then goes back to sleep. We talk some more until I've finished my second beer and suddenly I don't feel like getting drunk anymore. I'm thinking, I might just head back into work.

"Thanks," I say to the guy in the truck.

I hop out of the cab then stand still, looking over the hospital as the dust settles from the tires. The place is looking pristine and calm. It's as if the hospital is glimmering now. I walk to the sidewalk and watch bees in the flowerbed. I can really smell those flowers. I walk the path to the side entrance then fumble with my key in the lock. When I step inside, I hear voices. The sound is not quiet, the cheerful welcome I was hoping for, but it will do. I look down the hall, squinting in the dark, and can see the nurse and doctor. They're coming down the hall with a younger guy in a wheelchair. The guy in the chair looks pretty healthy. He looks around as he passes the rooms. The doctor and nurse see me as they turn, but they don't say anything and they don't frown. I don't even think they knew I was gone. I'm given a lot of leverage at this place, so I guess it's alright to take off now and then. I walk in and join the fray. They're helping the new guy into a bed.

"Can I help?" I ask, eager to get started.

"Sure," the nurse says. "He speaks French, so you can be our translator."

I speak French better than any of the nurses here. I seem to have a way with languages.

"Bonjour, je m'appelle John Zhukov," I say to the guy. "Comment ça va?"

"Ça va," he says.

"Would you like anything?" I ask in French.

He shakes his head.

"Non."

The nurse says, "Can you ask him if he'd like to try a new drug which might help him with his AIDS infection, Zhukov?"

"I...um." I'm not sure what to think about that. I'm still feeling good, but her request sort of throws me.

I look at him, then translate.

He thinks about it, then looks up with a smile.

"Oui. Merci. Oui." He says it looking pretty happy. I'm thinking it's more naive than anything, the way he answered so quickly. I stand my ground and say what I'm going to, no matter what.

"The drugs can be dangerous," I say to him in French. "Some patients die from the drugs."

I give a quick glance to the nurse. She probably caught what I said but the doctor's French is horrible. The nurse just nods to him, confirming my statement.

Now we're both watching him. He seems to pause. Then he smiles again, this time bigger than the last.

"J'aime le médicaments."

I like the medication? What did that mean? Now I'm starting to wonder if he understands what I meant, or if he really understands what I'm talking about.

I try to explain it to him again. I'm taking it slow so he gets every word, but he gives an odd reaction the moment I'm done speaking. He just sort of shrugs, then smiles oddly.

Is he alright? Does he really speak French that well? I think he does.

The doctor hands him his clipboard with the consent form on it. The guy seems to understand what it's for, because he signs it with the pen. Then he hands it back to the doctor with a cheerful nod. The doctor seems more sombre. The big smile is gone from his face. But he's set on what he's doing, *nonetheless*. There's a cold wind about, a haze of sternness, sights locked firmly on a destination. Whether by the road to hell, or the road to reason, he'll get there one way or the other.

The doctor walks off. He's left the nurse and me in an awkward bind. It's filled with a furtiveness not conveyed by speech. Speech would only lessen the awkwardness.

"What drug are you administering?" I ask. She's not looking at me. She's not looking at the patient either. Her lips are pursed in a prudent expression of disagreement and conflict.

"I think it's Nevidil," she says, then walks off. I don't watch her go.

I was feeling fine, I think. I was happy. Now I'm just standing here over his bed. My shoulders feel slumped. It's like I was hit with a brick in the face. Hit on a day which was starting to turn around. I look up at the guy. He has his head back on the pillow. His eyes are closed and his mouth is open, a perfectly content expression on his face. I open my mouth to say something, but nothing comes. I walk away and I don't know what I'll do.

Maybe see more patients.

"Are we sure these people need new treatments?" I ask.

Dr. Parkston is behind his desk again, flipping over an old coin in his hand. He looks towards the wall, but I think he's watching me. Lazy particles of dust float through the air, like fireflies. I'm beginning to dislike this office.

"Imagine a world with no drug testing on humans, Zhukov." He says it lightly now, like he's really on to something. "Imagine if we couldn't get approval for those drugs, and later in history, maybe a thousand years later, we find out that millions died because we weren't willing to sacrifice a few. Take the ants, a wise group of insects. When one of their number becomes sick, they carry it far away from the collective and leave it there to die. Not out of malice, but out of a desire to save thousands more. To save the masses. How foolish would we be as a human race if we did not take hold of the opportunities available. Oh, nobody, not even me—do you think I like this? No. Absolutely not. Nobody wants to test these drugs on humans. But someone has to. That's part of what it means to be a leader. To be a doctor even. To make the hard choices. I am the little secret that people like to stuff into their closet and forget about. Oh, they may condemn us in public, but privately, you bet your ass they want us out here, doing our job, and making sure that when they get sick they'll have all the treatment opportunities available."

"But why in Africa? Why don't we do it in America? Why does it seem like we're doing these tests on people with fewer options and less understanding of their rights instead of doing this in North America?"

Dr. Parkston shakes his head, like the facts made him angry.

"Don't ask me that question. Ask somebody higher in the food chain. This is where the job is for now and somebody decided that. The Western World likes to believe they are perfectly moral. That they have gained a superiority over lesser nations. When in fact, they are the ones exploiting those nations. They send blankets one day and send bombs the next. It is a love/hate relationship. They are doing a lot of good and a lot of wrong. People don't like to think about it. I wouldn't either. But this is the job. This is where the war must be fought."

When the sun goes down I'm not sure I'll live with myself. This isn't suicide I'm talking about. It's being free. Free from guilt. And I'm thinking, That's the worst time to worry; when darkness stretches over the land. When the moon spills silver onto the water-skin and the trees begin to sway. The night should be a time of reflection. A time of pleasant magic.

When I worry about myself I wonder if doubt will drag me to hell, or if it will be my actions that will take me. Destruction is before the sinners, and so I have wandered a beach. The tide is coming up and I can feel the water washing in and I know if I don't get out I'll drown! But I'm not sure if I want to leave, or can. And maybe if I stay it will all be alright. Maybe I'll learn to swim. I should turn and run but apathy is heavy.

I place her folder in the cupboard with the cigarettes. Then I sit down on the sofa and watch television. It's like playing a happy song to a widow whose husband has just died—if she cares.

I look at the time on the clock. It tells me it's 3:50 PM. The clock counts out the seconds quickly. When the countdown's finished I'll have to face the music. But not yet. I walk out of the staff lounge then start up the hall. I turn towards Doctor Parkston's office, then I knock twice.

"Come in."

I turn the knob. Parkston is reading a piece of paper. He has his head back slightly, a curl to his lip.

He looks up, and the look fades.

"Ah, Zhukov. How can I help you?"

"I was wondering if we could talk."

"Please."

He seems gracious, and reflective now. I stride to the chair and sit.

"I was wondering about the new patient," I say immediately. "We're giving him Nevidil?"

"Yes."

"Is the drug dangerous?"

"It's new," he says professionally, "but it's not dangerous. Some patients can have a bad reaction. I doubt that he'll have a bad reaction to the drug. The chances of that happening are slim. Maybe 20 percent."

"But he seems fine," I say. My voice comes out whiney.

"Hmm," he says. It's an odd expression. Unexpected. He puts down the paper then takes tissue from his pocket, starts cleaning his glasses. Then slowly, he replaces the glasses on his face.

"I have to tell you, Zhukov. It's a hard choice. We're supposed to administer new drugs here. Do you know how many people die a year from AIDS? Take a guess."

"Probably fifty-thousand," I say as a guess.

"More like 1.8 million. That's a big number. And this hospital is the first defence against the AIDS virus. It is the cavalry charge against the virus. This is *war* in a way. In every war there will be casualties."

"But this is medicine," I say.

"Not like ordinary medicine. This is more like war. Really it is. If an invading nation came into the United States and killed one million people, what do you think we would do? Of course we would go to war with them. We might even send nuclear weapons. And in any war we would sacrifice our own soldiers to ensure the continuation of our nation. To ensure we won the war."

I nod. I'm not sure I get it completely.

"…Those people out there don't know their own importance. They are the soldiers. Us doctors, and you too, Zhukov…are the generals who send them into action. Some will make it and others will not."

"But they're not soldiers," I say, and I feel like I'm falling down a well. Doesn't anyone get this? Is it I who don't get it?

"Oh…but they are," Parkston says with some gravity. "They really are. They may not know it, but soldiers don't always know the purpose of their missions. They are laying down their lives when they have to, in hopes of living in peace later on. If they don't survive, then they know their children will live in peace. They know that later generations will honour their sacrifice."

"I see."

"I hope you do. This is an important war. The modern era has given way to a new form of threat: the virus. The virus is the small killer which is mightier than any foreign army. It kills without discrimination. It knows nothing of the Geneva Convention, or of mercy. It takes women and children. Old men and old women. Mothers, daughters, grandfathers, grandmothers, fathers, sons, passers-by, and the wanderers."

I'm having some trouble following him. I can partially see what he's saying. But I really don't like it.

"It's the greatest enemy we know. Oh, in the developed nations we like to sit back and make our judgements while the war goes on in some other land. It touches us, but barely. Being a doctor is making the hard choices. You can't fight an illness unless you're prepared to do whatever it takes to win. It's merely a numbers game, Zhukov. I hope you see that. We must sacrifice a few to save thousands, millions more. Every general knows that. Even the lowly lieutenant knows about sacrifice. It is the burden of great men and smaller men. It is what being human is boiled down to."

I nod again. Maybe I just want him to think I'm agreeing with everything.

"When we learn to wake up to the war around us, we can fight it better. Until then we must fight in secret to protect the happy masses who live in ignorance of the perils which are lurking in the dark. I am society's darkest secrets. The necessary ones which have been put away in the closet. And AIDS is the secret war. All diseases are society's secret war."

When I'm out near the jungle I see a group of monkeys. They're always around, and ready to torment me. They are in some kind of playful mood today, as they look down at me then smile. It's with a note of manic cynicism I'd expect from the jolly city-dweller. One of them grabs a mango, and throws it where I'm standing. I take a step to one side to avoid the fruit crossfire.

I walk home from the hospital every day, and often stop to watch wildlife. The monkeys, while perhaps much like humans, do not seem overly human to me. They seem too jocund and carefree; even reckless. What is it about monkeys that some people find so human? It is in looks and genetic similarity, but hardly. With many, it is in personality and in behaviour. And if it is in behaviour, I don't see it readily. I certainly hope we humans would not be so reckless, but of course, are not humans really animals in many ways? And there is a question

I have always pondered. What makes a man sentient really? What makes him self-aware?

I tell myself as I'm watching these monkeys that man is no more self-aware than the animals, and that this idea that man is more aware than the animals only proves that man is less aware than his vain ego would lead him to believe. For it seems very egotistical and arrogant to me, that man should think because he is smarter that he is in fact more aware. Where is the proof for it?!

Do not man and beast both have a desire to live? Do not both have to adapt to their environments in order to survive? Surely man is smarter. I have never seen a monkey do calculus. Perhaps monkeys have been shown to have superior memory, but then, memory is not intelligence. A book, a piece of paper, has ultimate memory, but no one would say that a piece of paper is intelligent, or that it's even alive! And why is it that men who have much knowledge are regarded as intelligent? Is it not how they use knowledge which proves their intelligence? Or let me ask, how good are they at problem solving? An encyclopedia contains much knowledge, but it is just a book. And a book is not intelligent. It is just paper. It cannot build anything. It can dispense facts, but it cannot put these facts together to solve a problem or advance. It takes an intelligent human being to read the pages and put the knowledge to good use: through understanding.

As I look at these monkeys in the trees I think perhaps they are indeed more intelligent than some PhDs, who, being unable to advance their own field, simply fill themselves with hate. Would these pseudo-professors be able to survive in the wild? Would they be able to learn which fruits to eat and which not to? Would they be so foolish with their vain egos that they would encounter a creature greater than themselves and pick a fight and be torn to shreds?

Even the animals, I think, possess enough wisdom to preserve their own species. Though they might not be wise, they, as a species, do not perish by foolishness alone, given that conditions remain the same by which they might live. But haven't many species gone extinct? Died from the inability to adapt?

I am thinking these thoughts when something terrifying happens. It is like in those stories where a man has gone mad and doesn't know it. A monkey looks down from his perch. He's biting into a mango, juice dripping down his chin, then says, "Would you like a mango?"

I'm stunned.

"No, thank you," I say.

"They're quite good really. You ought to try one."

"I've had one before."

"Oh really."

"How can you talk?"

The monkey shrugs.

"Why does man never listen? You're listening now. I can see that you have problems on your plate, and that is a tricky thing for man. We animals do not concern ourselves with the great problems. We rely on reason, but we never stray into anything evil that our genes do not allow."

And before the conversation can pick up, I turn and start running as fast I can. I want to get away from that monkey and his talk. That monkey has nothing good to tell me. Nothing good to say to me! He's just trying to play a trick on me. I'm running towards the hospital at full speed. I don't look back until I'm inside.

I walk around the hospital while I'm thinking it through, and I know they'll administer the drug soon. I was in to check on the new guy earlier, and boy, he was just lying back. I don't think he knew what was coming down the pipe. I tried to speak reason to him, but he just seemed off. Maybe worse than me in some way. I wonder if he really is crazy, or out of touch. He sort of shrugged again to my warning as I adamantly explained the dangers and tried to get some common sense going. He couldn't be convinced otherwise, and boy, that just really upset me.

So now I'm standing by the door, looking out through glass, trying to put the new guy away, hoping I don't see any more monkeys. It's not that the monkey wasn't pleasant when he spoke. It's just that he was in my head. I'm not *that crazy* to not know when I'm actually crazy. But I must be going crazy, even though I can't afford to check myself in. I've got these thoughts in my head and the night is coming. When the night comes I'll have to live with myself, but I don't know how it will be yet.

I think, 1.8 million deaths a year. Maybe more than that. 34 million people living with AIDS, the doctor said. It's a tragedy. A silent genocide. And we have to stop it. But at what price? That's always the question. When you believe in God, you think these questions will be easy. The Bible lays out laws for you and you follow. But what kind of moral conundrum is this? It's a flawed human problem.

If I was human, I'd just help the guy escape. I'd do it when no one was looking. I'd make sure this couldn't happen again. I'd really take action. But I'm not human now—I'm starting to turn into a calculator. 1.8 million. Think of all the sons and daughters. It's almost unimaginable! I walk away from the door then start up the halls. The light is starting to fade from the sky when I enter the ICU.

He's awake now and eating soup.

"Bonjour. Vous souvenez-vous de moi?"

"Oui."

He smiles.

"Comprenez-vous ce que j'ai dit des médicaments?"

He shrugs.

"Oui."

Then he takes a big spoonful of soup and slurps it. He seems like a nice guy, but it's hard to read him.

When I walk away my head is swimming and I'm pretty frustrated. They'll be bringing his medication soon. I can count down the seconds. I don't have much time. I walk to the staff lounge and watch television. A documentary about Hiroshima, Nagasaki, and Osaka. They're showing all this footage of atom bombs exploding. It's getting to be that time, I think. It's nearly too late.

I won't do it. But I have to. Otherwise I'll *no longer* be human. I can't be a general. I'm not cut out to be general and *I don't have to be* a general. My head is swimming and blinding my vision. I'm really pacing before I have that thought: *A flame shooting up the wall. A fire truck whining and skidding around the bend.* I walk to the nurses' station and see the door ajar. Nobody's in there. I suppose it's time. I walk in, see they've got a big trash can; lots of papers. I rub my fingers together, then look around. My brow has broken out in a sweat. I wipe my forehead then gulp. I pick paper out of the bin. It's some kind of test result, and I think: that won't do.

Why oh why, does it have to be me? Why not some other poor sap? Why did it happen to me? I was just crazy. Young and reckless. Young and foolish. Young and lustful and over-obsessed with the female body; just like many other young men. Trying to find the answers like others around me, but failing miserably because I didn't want to know. I am like one of those schmucks in Austin, Texas who sit around, just as hopeless and shallow as the next, trying to find the answers to their existence. And here I stumble onto an assiduous conundrum!

I was raised in Russia to age 5, a polite little boy with a bad temper, and a condition most commonly called 'Crazy'. How am I any different? Why did I have to be the lab rat? Why did the world have to *fuck me over?* The doctors had me in some kind of experiment. Boy, they really did a number. I'm sure they only made it worse. But they've all got papers to write and Nobel prizes to win and I was just the next specimen in the long line of zoo animals, the mysterious puzzle to be unravelled, the knot which would make them king of Asia. Only the Gordian knot, which was me, was slashed rather than untied. I was like something to be conquered with the sword of the thermometer and the notebook and question.

But for now, I live with regret. It's like an itching in the skull, moving to the eye where the lid twitches and little men tickle my cornea. I know they're in there. I can hear them working through the clapboard, cracks opening in the psyche, sounds splayed and spattered across frontal lobes like a fumbling of wet paint; an odd locution, the construction crew with jackhammers, and cranes, and bulldozers, and shovels and little cranes so small you'd need a microscope to spot 'em. They're making jokes and groaning; implacable sounds. Which is why it's so unsatisfactory.

I close my eyes briefly, but I can hear them now, loquacious buggers with slavish tenacity, pulling at the strings like the puppet master at Pinocchio.

'Work hard, men! Keep it going! Don't back down! Don't give an inch!' Then their voices fade like a car under-ground. The radio signal's gone...for now.

Sometimes I see them.

Sometimes they see me. But not today.

There's a plaque with names in a scrawl so you'll remember. They want you to remember the generous. They want you to remember the blessed ones. Bless these saints of good-will and fortune. That's what the plaque says, and I remember every word—every letter, every accent of the names as if they were relatives. But I don't care. I couldn't care less about these people. These pseudo-saints in black robes, holding up their cheques in front of cameras. Oh, for all the good they do for themselves! The image it gives their company. And to think this is considered generosity. Am I supposed to feel grateful? Grateful for what?! Yeh, I'm indignant. In-dig-nation. It's coming out of my multiloquent pores. It's fuming out through my prolix breath, and seeping like an adipic syrup from my ears. I want to find them and shake their hands, then slap them into reality. *Remember the ones who gave.*

Did they do it so the oppressed might rise? Might live in harmony with the industrial world?

They got a tax break. They got a boost in sales and free advertising and a whole room of people had to be there to clap. They built a hospital to treat the people who couldn't be treated this way in North America. If they were treated this way here, it would raise eyebrows. It would cause the media to go into a frenzy like a fire-storm coming down from the hills.

I've thought it looked strange to have a hospital like this. So new. In rural Cameroon, which is where I am now, it looks plain bizarre. I want to scream, but it's a funny desire. I want to stamp my feet as I did when I was 5, being dragged to places I didn't want to go, strapped into a car-seat with seatbelts like handcuffs. I want to throw eggs and make the doctors lick it up. To trample the flowerbed—even those flowers—and tear down the building till the living things rise. We have goat herders a few miles south and I can see them like ants or wavy liquid shapes. I doubt they know what this place is. I doubt the screams frighten their herds into stampedes—and I wonder then if they'd even take notice.

I'm quite morbid, you know, and that's how I'm thinking. That's what people say. "Zhukov, there's something wrong with that child." The teachers in school couldn't figure me out, and neither could the doctors. They asked questions 'til they were blue in the face. They thought I was violent. They thought— one did—I was a sociopath. I told him it hurt my feelings and he just made a face. Ugly man. He wore a suit jacket with a ruffled shirt collar and has an unkempt beard. When he spoke, it was like molasses being poured through a trombone. He simply nodded to my breaking heart and 'Mmhmm'd' and scratched down a note like I'd said something interesting. I don't understand it.

It's like the recipe got botched.

Like the egg in the ovary had too much yeast and the wrong things rose till they baked up subconscious. The doctors said I don't know what's acceptable. That I don't know what to say. I end up spilling it out like a body from a coffin. Guests shocked, faces white. Old women clutching their canes and babies weeping at the hideous sight. Make the bad man go away! Make the crazy one invisible! And just like that I'm invisible. That's me, though, popping out of the box. Saying hello to everyone. Then put me back in and bury me. Bury me so deep you won't even remember.

I can imagine 'em piling the dirt up. They're piling it high like the Tower of Babel.

But the people are nice in their sociopathic way. Most smile. Most of them try—or say they try—to make the world better. I don't believe it. It's selfish, I think. Me, me, me! They're trying to keep their children clothed. That's the furthest their selflessness goes, and I'm the sick one for *trying to be honest*? For saying that I don't give a fuck what happens? Because I don't believe in the system? I don't believe in the morality of the Western World and their boasting self-righteousness and their sadistic immorality disguised as love for fear of being judged. The hospital is what you should know about—not the people. The people built the place, and if you want to know something then you'll know about the hospital and get more of the story. The place is a paved nature conservation and it's got a strip mall on top. It's a research hospital where people get medicine and drugs, but there's a difference. The drugs haven't been tested—the medicine has. Drugs which are sure to have odd reactions like when you make fire by igniting bubbles and you don't know what you're actually doing. It just happens and it's either cool or scary. Scientists have blown themselves up playing around, and that's about the perfect picture in my mind. Only we're blowing away the poor guy. The guy who's got no choice but to come here and try and take our drugs or take no drugs at all. It's legal, and I've learned it is more than that.

I am just an employee, another schmuck, a high school dropout with a thermometer instead of a crack pipe. I'm the guy who works the middle ground, peddling between.

There's a world of sorrow and world of medicine. I'm a postal worker delivering letters to people too sick to come to the door. Some letters, anthrax, others, healing. Both items appearing and smelling alike, but some don't know which 'til it's in.

We feed 'em crimicide, and femicide, like we were committing bovicide and nothing near a homicide. Cattle coming through the gate for slaughter. One silent genocide matched by another.

I'm a postal worker, not a general.

The logic is simple. The choices are clear.

I have to be a general, and to win the war I must identify the enemy. I walk to the supply room and open the door. We've got a lot of needles in this place. I really need a needle to do this next part. I've used a needle on myself and I know that it's painless. A small little pinch, then the drug takes effect. That's what this has to be: painless. For him and for me. I walk to the shelf and take down a syringe, then I take down a bottle of morphine. I take the syringe out of its package and look at the needle tip. *The needle makes a hole and through the hole the dreams enter.* The needle is the sword of the medical staffer. I fill the syringe with morphine, then place the bottle in my pocket and put the plastic cap back on. I stuff the needle into my pocket, then sit down on a box of medical supplies, and I hurt all over. My heart is pounding in my chest, and I know that I have to breathe slowly. I've never done this before, but it has to be done. I have to be a general. I have to eliminate the virus. I think there is an enmity building up in my gut. It's causing my hands to shake as I work. It's causing me to act.

I was sitting in the audience like all the others. I heard the tall man speaking at the lectern. He was talking about AIDS and vaccines and cures. There was some applause. I found myself hanging on every word. This was my first meeting with Doctor Parkston, a visitor to York University. I was studying nursing and I was getting kicked out. They were still discussing it but I knew they would do it. When a student steals drugs from the clinic there's only one thing the school will do in most cases and that's give the offender permission to leave with a strong scolding for erring. I was trying to use drugs to cure myself. I was practicing drug testing on myself. I almost went into a coma at one point and that's how they found me: in a pool of vomit. When they found the drugs in my room and realized I was the one who'd been stealing, things were undoubtedly grim. But they allowed me a trial because I was crazy. I received that much decency at least. I liked to think that I was on a roll in the matter of finding ways to fail.

After the lecture I saw the tall doctor in the hall and I spoke to him about his craft. He seemed pleased to see me. It was as if he was already working it out in his head, that this student would somehow be a prodigy of sorts. I found myself explaining my entire story to him. I expressed great interest in his work. I really was interested and thought, maybe, if I get the chance to complete my degree, I will one day be able to work with him.

"That's a very interesting story, Mr. Zhukov," Parkston had said. "Perhaps if things go badly, we can work something out regardless."

And that's exactly what happened in the end. Some good things can come to an end and at those times bad things can commence. A week later I was no longer a student and a month later I was on the phone with Doctor Parkston. We were talking about Cameroon. I can imagine I owe a debt of gratitude to the man. But then, I think, I was still on a roll.

I step out of the supply room and look up the hall. Everything seems to have taken on darkness. I just need to kill, I think. I don't need to murder. If it's murder, it will be a murder by accident. I'm just killing like in wartime. I'm just executing the criminal who will kill again. And it's only because the criminal will kill again that I must. I walk down the hall and knock on the door. I've been knocking on this door most of the day.

"Come in." Parkston's voice sounds happy now. I'm not sure if I should feel guilty or feel angry. What business does he have being happy? What business do I have to be angry? Let him be happy, I think. This should be more pleasant for him than for me.

I enter and close the door behind me.

He looks up at me.

"Ah, hello Zhukov. How are you doing now?"

I nod.

"I'm fine doctor. I was just wondering…um…is this going to end?"

"End?"

"The drug testing. I was just thinking…maybe we should quit doing it."

"Oh that again, Zhukov? I really don't think I can explain it enough times, but I'll explain it again. This really does have to be done."

It does have to be done.

It's as if he were really speaking to me now. It's like he's telling me what to do. I have to obey.

Parkston gets up and comes around his desk, then sits on the desk so that he can talk to me better.

"I know this is hard for you, Zhukov. It's hard to make the big choices. But the big choices have to be made."

"I think you're right, doctor. But I don't want to do it."

"You have to do it. If you don't, many more people will die."

I think I feel my eyes beginning to well up with tears. I reach in my pocket and pull out the syringe then take the cap off.

"What are you doing?" Parkston says. He sounds hesitant now. He looks at the syringe.

"I have to do it. I know that now." And there are tears coming down my face. A tear traces my cheek then patters on my lap. I stand up.

"Zhukov, is everything alright? I think you're hallucinating again." Parkston starts for the door but I'm there behind him. I grab him from behind and place a hand over his mouth. With the other hand I stick the needle in his neck. It doesn't go in as gently as I'd like. He cringes a little, but I feel relieved. I depress the plunger. I watch the liquid enter his body. He throws himself back and we go to the floor. My hand is still over his mouth and I'm gripping his face so that his skin blanches white. There's a muffled scream. His feet are thrashing as he tries to get leverage. He's walking himself around in a circle. *Oh doctor, why did you make me do this!? Why!* There are tears on my face. "I don't want to," I say. I'm crying as we thrash on the floor and the hollow sobs fill up the room. I want him to be calm. I want him to stop. And then he does. His feet kick slightly and are still. His arms relax and fall to the floor. I feel his body go limp on top of me like a fish out of water clinging to consciousness; clinging to the last bits of life as darkness envelops him. He's going to sleep. *Sleep doctor. Sleep.* I inch myself out from under him, then fill the syringe again. The struggle is over, the hard part is ahead of me. I pause in calmness then look down at his body. He looks peaceful. He's sleeping like a man who had lain down and for some reason decided to take a nap. A second dose will kill, I realize. Now is the moment, I decide. And I wonder, *Is it too late to go back?*

I exit the room then start down the hallway. I get to the staff lounge, where I pull down her folder which I've stashed in the cupboard for light reading. I start pacing the room again in a fit of anxiety. I can hear those monkeys but I need them to stop. I'm getting worried now. Worried about the future.

I hear the sound of a bird scratching at the window. They've got curtains in the room and a big plastic trash bin. Two things I'll need, and I almost wish they weren't there. It's like a knife leading me on. As if King Duncan was dead on the carpet and Macbeth was pacing the TV lounge. I take the lid off the trash, then look inside: papers, candy wrappers, left-over muffins, all of these scrunched up and forgotten. It will have to do, I decide at last. I open up the folder and look at the picture. She's lying on the bed in the ICU, but someone took a picture of her for the file. It's a memorial shot, I think. I pull the borrowed lighter from my pocket, remove the Polaroid, then flick the flint. I hold the flame up under the picture then watch as the corner starts to burn. I watch as the woman's face lights up. Her whole body goes up in a laughing orange.

The edge starts to curl. The flame grows great. A black smoke is rising towards the ceiling like a smoke line on the prairie. I drop the burning Polaroid in the garbage, then stand back. Actions are easy, I think. I feel relieved. I take out her test results then crumple them up. I throw them on the flame. A smoke's rising up like a barbeque cookout.

Then I remember something. I look up to the smoke detector on the ceiling. My heart skips a beat.

I panic.

I grab a chair and slide it over, then clamber up as fast as I can. I grab at the plastic but the lid won't budge. I'm straining my fingers to pry that lid off. This chair is too short; that's the problem. I reach as hard as I can. I stand on my tippy toes, then I give it a hard yank and the lid comes off and hits the floor. I remove the battery and step back down. The smoke is pouring up like a campfire now. I watch the flames leap out of the bin, then I walk to the cupboard, listening to them crackle. I take down a pack of smokes from the cupboard. I slide a cigarette out and light it. The smoke's getting thick as I watch the fire. I take a pull on my cigarette. The smoke feels good in my lungs. I walk to the bin and slide it to the curtains.

They're thin white curtains. Somebody paid money for these curtains.

I grab the curtains, then drape them over the trash bin so the flames are touching the fabric. Then I take a step back, and watch, waiting for it to come to its final conclusion. My big plan.

Operation start-a-fire.

The curtains catch and a flame shoots up. I flick my cigarette to the floor, then I step out and close the door behind me. The halls are silent and dark as I move. I listen as I walk with the world pressing in. A telephone's ringing from somewhere nearby. A nurse is talking in a chatty voice. I'm walking quickly to the ICU. When I enter, I can see all the nurses working. A patient coughs beside me then wheezes. I wait 'til I'm standing in the middle of the room. Then I let 'em have it, "FIRE! There's a FIRE in the staff lounge! FIRE! FIRE!"

The head nurse hurries over in a fluster. Her arms just waving around as she walks.

"Where?!" she asks, with trembling lips.

"The staff lounge. It's pretty bad." I try to sound like it's surprising to me, but I can imagine everyone seeing through the facade.

The nurses hurry around in a panic. Just then, a fire alarm goes off.

RIIIIINNNGGGGGGGGGG!!!

"Is that a fire?"

"There's a fire!" the nurse yells to everyone. "We need to get everybody out of here, now!"

I'm running. I run to the supply room and see the wheelchairs stacked amongst mops and brooms. I grab a chair and unfold it. Then I shoot out of the room and start tearing down the hall. When I get to a room, I hurry in. I see the guy who was thirsty. He's still lying on the bed sleeping soundly. I put a hand on his shoulder to wake him. He opens his eyes and looks at me. He looks startled. I think he can see the urgency in my face. Who wouldn't? If not, he can sure hear that alarm ringing.

"Zhukov?" he says meekly over the noise.

"There's a fire," I say. "I have to get you out of here until the fire trucks put the flames out."

"O.K.," he says, and he looks a little worried. Boy, I feel guilty for that look.

I angle the wheelchair then slide him off the bed and help him get settled. He's still pretty strong. Strong enough to sit down so I don't have to lift him. Too tall for me to manage, if I had to. Once in the chair, we take off. There's nurses working fast, flying up and down the hall in a panic. The head nurse wheels the new guy out, and we almost collide at the door. There's no time to say sorry, so we just keep going.

When we're at the back door I angle it open then use the doorstop to keep it clear. The nurse heads out and I follow. I'm out the door into the fading light now. The air feels cool and crisp on my skin. We head out onto the grass, then I park near the trees and wait for a moment. I have to think of what I just did. But that will come later, when there's more time. I watch as wheelchairs head out into the sun, then I hear the fire trucks coming from afar. It's a whine over the jungle, far away, but audible. I ask the guy if he's alright, then I head back in to get more patients. The smoke starts coming around the corner, now. It's getting tough to see.

As the smoke is stinging my eyes, I pray and hope that I won't have to live with myself.

We all watch as they douse the flames. The head nurse reports they got all the patients out. There's only one person missing, she says. Doctor Parkston is unaccounted for. She took a tally five minutes ago and seemed concerned for his absence.

Where did Parkston go?

Is he somewhere else that we can't see?

Everyone is watching the building in awe. Those barely conscious have tried to watch but there's hardly anything to see. Just flames and smoke and the sun slipping down, as a soft breeze picks up and tussles our hair. The firefighters went in with oxygen masks. That was some time ago, but I assume they're alright. They have to check everything out. I saw them go in one by one with their axes in hand and their face shields down.

By now, the flames are starting to die. I can see 'em making progress as they scurry about. The water is winning. A thick smoke is billowing up into the sky but it's dying. The nurse's lips are pursed as we huddled together. We're all just watching the fireworks show. My patient looks out of it. I lean over and feel his pulse, but his pulse is fine. He's just really weak. This will all be alright, I think. We'll move him to the other hospital and set him up there. At that place, they use real medicine. At that place they actually heal.

I'm watching the progress and am slightly disappointed. I'm a little sorry they got the flames out so quickly. Partly, I was hoping the whole building would be gone. I wasn't sure how long it would take but they build the structures out of concrete and steel. It doesn't burn quickly and the firefighters are quick. They could have been slower and if they'd only known, they might have slowed down, I think. I look at the fire truck parked out front. A firefighter is directing things with hand motions. The guy seems more relaxed than before. I want to tell him, 'I was hoping the whole hospital would burn', 'Maybe you could take it easy.', 'Maybe if you only turned off the water'.

A couple firefighters come strolling out, and they've got a man on a stretcher who's not moving. What's this now? The man's wearing a white coat. As they move aside, I recognize his face. It's Doctor Parkston! They lay him down on the grass, then one of the firefighters starts CPR. The head nurse rushes over but I'm too scared to move. They're pumping at his chest, until they stop. *Don't stop!* I'm thinking. *Keep trying!* But a firefighter removes his mask, then looks up to the head nurse and shakes his head tragically, like they do in the movies. *No,* I'm thinking. *That wasn't supposed to happen.* He doesn't have a burn on him! Keep trying!

Smoke inhalation.

No, it's not that. It's morphine. An overdose of morphine. But how do I know this. How do I know that he didn't die in the fire.

Morphine.

Overdose.

Murder.

The word comes to me from the back of my mind. What was he doing in there? Why didn't he get out? No, I think. I keep repeating the word 'no' over and over. I'll have to live with myself and I didn't want to. But I'm not just responsible. I'm *directly responsible.* Everything is tumbling. Everyone seems to move in slow motion. I brush a tear from my eye. The water from the fire-canon seems slow to look at. The smoke pouring up seems stuck in the sky. I follow the smoke line up and up and for a moment I'm carried on the wings of birds, and then, in a moment, I'm thrown back to earth.

We've loaded the last of the patients, then the last ambulance turns around the bend. The siren whines then it's gone from sight on its way to the other hospital. That's when I see the police by the plaque. They're talking to the janitor and they've got their heads down. They're taking notes. The janitor's still got his broom in his hand like he's about to mop if he could find a place. Mr. Omji shoots a few looks in my direction and I can't help but think that he looks kind of sad. *And who wouldn't be?* I think. I wonder what they're talking about, but I don't really care. I'm kicking around, really upset. To be honest, I'm not sure what I'll do. I just killed a guy, is what I'm thinking. The police are right there and I know what to do. This decision is easy.

The last rays of light slip out under the earth and I can see by all the headlights that the nurses are leaving. They're going to their cars and they're in a hurry. They're heading home for the night and they'll be back in a week. I'm just kicking around when two officers start walking. One is tall and the other is squat. The taller officer looks concerned. They seem serious as they come towards me.

"John Zhukov?" the taller one says to me. He's got his notebook handy to take down a testimony.

"Yes," I say.

"Mr. Omji says he saw you in the staff lounge just before the fire started."

I nod.

"I started the fire," I say firmly. "It was my fault."

They look at each other with shock. A few cars drive past and head out to the road.

The taller officer shakes his head tragically. Then he looks off, as if to say, *I've seen too much in this job.*

Then he looks at me with a sombre expression and I see compassion in his eyes when he says, "I'm sorry, young man. We're going to have to place you under arrest."

PART III:
A CONSEQUENCE OF A HARD DECISION MADE

THE DOOR OPENS WITH a hard jolt and I'm pushed out into the yard, like a bag of garbage. This place is the land of languid suffering. I imagined something bad, but this is worse. I assess the mood immediately, and it isn't pretty. A few lights shine onto the prisoners about me who are living a life of gentle misery. The smell of urine is acrid, as is another smell which is human refuse. Prisoners are huddled in groups under tents, like mendicant travellers, lost from the road. I've seen stuff like this in movies, but I've never actually been physically close. Right now, I'm close enough to touch. I'm close enough to smell. I'm close enough to realize I'm a part of this…whatever it is. Where these people were going, I don't know.

I hear the sounds of groaning in the yard. Someone is weeping in the open space.

I am moving over bodies; people sleeping in the dark and piles of clothing and plastic wrappers. There's a man with a sheet, sprawled out on the dirt. He's trying to keep cool in the heat. I see his beard and his thick brown hair more clearly with each passing footstep. I step over him, and he stirs in the dark. It is strange to think this is where some sleep. In the dust. In the brutal conditions of nature. I come to a wall and place my hands on the brick like I might be able to push it aside. The wall feels warm under the tips of my fingers like tiny pinpricks of electricity. It probably gets hot during the day, I think, and I'm not looking forward to the morning. I look up and see high concrete walls, and a wrapping of razor wire.

A man starts shouting in Swahili.

There's a quick scuffle with three men by the wall, then it's over. The men go about their business, swearing under their breath, hate pouring off their backs. I sit by the wall. This is where I live now. This is where I'll be for some time—how long I'm not sure, but I imagine it will be a while. I imagine—not wanting to face the concept—that I'll probably die here.

It's dark and abysmal like an open tomb. The yard is the portrait of night. The night is the remainder of oppression which the sun beat back during the day—a sallow ponderous place, sufficiently cruel and abstract, and not very big, if you want to know. Bodies have been crammed in like cows. A cookfire burns out of a large metal bin from which smoke pours up into the estuary. I think, *This is what it means to be human. This is what it means to take action.* I lean my head back against the wall then close my eyes out of exhaustion, though it's hard to sleep with all this alien sound. But I only feel like sleeping now.

Now, after the death and the fire, after the questions and the choices, after years of being crazy and years of wishing I could turn back time.

I drift between wakefulness and sleep…and for the longest time, I hear sounds. A crackling of noise like a whip snapping—but it can't be a whip. A whisper or two, carrying through the walls. A slight yelp like a dog being struck. And ever so slowly…patiently, it begins to fade. It is like I am being sucked down a well. It drifts off further on the sea of sleep until sleep comes like a pleasant tide and dreams begin.

As I dream, *I'm in a meadow and I drink water from a stream. The sun is up but no longer hot. I see women and children on the horizon dancing on the hillside. I stop and look up at the trees which are swaying in the breeze. I think, this is not the present. This is a simpler time. An older time with easier moral choices. The choice to hunt. The choice to be honest or lie. The choice to love your neighbour or commit murder. All these choices are clear and defined. The water is crisp and I lower myself into that cold water and let it take away my pain.*

I awake with a start. Someone is yelling mournfully. It's a hazy image at first which becomes more liquid. I tilt my head back, so it hurts my eyes. I have to squint to see through the haze.

As my eyes adjust I see I'm here. I haven't moved despite my dreams. In the daytime the place takes on more definition. It's harder to bear, I think.

I have to focus now.

People are lying in a scattering of flies. Three men are gambling by the wall. There's a box between them where they lay their cards. A man is coughing from where he lies. It sounds like bronchitis. I focus on him. He's an older man with grey hair. His skin is dark as obsidian. His features are gaunt and pathetic and pushing the limits of biology. He's lying flat on his back in the sun with that baking heat on his face and arms. His khakis are torn and his shoes are gone—probably stolen, I think. I can even see that his toes are bloody.

I get up slowly and walk to him, then kneel down and look him over. I'm like the medical staffer I once was. This guy has deep lines in his face and there's a cut on his cheek below the eye. I grab his hand gently with my own 'cause I want him to know I'm a friend.

"Are you alright?" I ask in French.

The man looks up at me wearily. After a moment's pause, he says, "Ça va. I can't be helped now, young lad."

He looks away.

"What's wrong?"

He tells me. I almost knew that would be the answer. It had to be almost as cruel to me as it would be to him. And I think of the AIDS clinic, and feel a moment's remorse.

"How long have you been here?" I ask.

He looks up and closes his eyes and his mouth moves like he's really thinking. Then he opens them again.

"Four days."

Only four days, I think. And already he will probably die. If I could just get out of here; just pick him up and rush him to the clinic, we could probably save him. But now I'm stuck. I look around for a guard, thinking someone has to help him. But I don't see any guards. There's only one steel door which leads into this yard, and the door is closed. I look up at the sun. It's hot. So hot you could cook an egg in the dust. I look at the guy. I can't just let him lie here and die. There's a good shade by the wall to my right, but it's a long ways to drag a guy who's really sick.

"Would you like some shade?" I ask him.

He nods.

"Alright," I say. He's emaciated from lack of food. He's really going to be lighter than normal. I try to weigh him in my mind before we take action. He's about 6-2. I think about it. He won't be impossible to carry. I pull him up slowly and wrap his arm around my shoulder. I try to do the work 'cause he's too sick to help. I drag him as he tries to walk. He's heavier than I thought. I have to really strain to keep him balanced. We manoeuvre around people lying in the dirt. I get to the wall. I lay him down gently. It must be a hundred degrees cooler here. After he's settled, I kneel over him. I look into his face. He's moving his lips, and his eyes are closed, but I think he's doing better.

"Is it better?" I ask, just to make sure.

"Better."

Much better, is what I think. I sit against the wall and just let out a sigh. The prison yard is nearly static. I'm watching the day unfold.

When I open my eyes again, the man isn't moving. I crawl slowly, feeling stiff. I move along the dirt like a snake. I stop over him on all fours. I look into his face like there's a puzzle to be solved. Then I study his features for something. It's something I can't put into words but can recognize. His eyes are closed, like the man in the drawer.

But that seems like so long ago. I reach up to his neck and feel for a pulse. It's gone; gone from this world. I sit back against the wall. A single tear traces my check and falls on my lap. Should I apologize now? Should I bang on the door?

The door to the yard swings open. Three guards step outside while another stands watch. The man standing watch is holding a shotgun. He's frowning at the prisoners, who don't bother to look. The men playing cards don't even stop. The guards carry rifles, glimmering black in the sun as they move. I think of efficient workers; efficient bees, flapping and buzzing like they didn't know what they were doing. They start looking around. I watch as they start rolling people over. They begin scanning the yard in quick furtive gestures. A guard with dreadlocks points to me.

What's this all about? Can't a man get a little peace to mourn for the dead?

All three come over, stepping lightly. One keeps watch while the other two speak. Maybe I'm dehydrated, but I feel like they're talking to someone else; like it's happening at a distance, instead of right in front of me. They want me to come. They need me to get up.

I explain that the man beside me is dead. A guard looks down at him with possible concern. He nods. He's a young guy with a note of goodness to him, but he also seems firm when he speaks.

"He'll be taken care of."

Like hell.

I explain I won't leave; not until I can see he's taken care of. All three of the guards look at each other, then the young guy looks back at me.

"He'll be taken care of. I promise. We don't leave the dead out here."

"I have your promise?"

"Yes," he says affectionately. "I assure you we would never do that."

I look around at the yard and all the prisoners wandering about in the sun. I'm suddenly angry.

"This place is pretty horrible," I say. "For people who say they'd never leave a dead guy to rot."

The guards seem unfazed by my defiance. They're waiting for me to get up but I'm mad now. I just want to hit someone I'm so mad, and maybe I want to cry. It's like I should be crying but the tears don't come despite how much it would fit for a funeral.

They want a clue. But I won't give it to them.

They don't seem upset but they look confused. I can't judge, I think. I never could, but I can't now. Not when I'm a murderer, I can't. And when I realize this, I calm down. I slowly get to my feet and brush dirt off. I look back at the man in the dust as we walk. We're winding our way through a maze of bodies, moving quickly until we're inside. It's like a tingling on my skin. It's cooler in here.

We turn up the first hall. The halls are green. Even the floors are green and I wonder whose bright idea that was. We reach this beaten-up door with '9' painted on. A guard opens it with a jangling key-ring. The door swings wide, and I see a middle-aged man. This man has slightly elegant features. He's sitting at a table with a cup of tea and a pot. I'm shoved inside. There's a punitive click as footsteps fade.

"Please sit down," the man says to me. He has sallow eyes; eyes deep and analytical. He's watching my every movement for some kind of tell.

I walk to the table and sit.

"Would you like some tea?" he asks politely. He motions towards the pot like a waiter. There are purple flowers painted on the side and up the handle. It seems an odd thing to see in a prison.

I nod.

"Yes," I say, because my mouth is dry.

He slowly grabs the kettle then pours a fresh cup. The sound of the liquid is oddly familiar. He slides the cup over and I grip it. I slowly take a sip and the tea tastes like flowers. Neither bitter nor sweet. Just some kind of flower has been ground up. I look up slowly to assess the man. I assume he's an officer, but I can't be sure. Maybe just someone looking for information. The man has three scars along his chin. The scar gives the appearance of a tiger attack, or that maybe, he himself, is a tiger. But I feel at ease. Despite his menacing features, he seems calm, not vicious. He leans back with a fluent motion, looks carelessly at the pot.

"We have been in contact with Amnesty International," he says slowly before taking a sip. "We did not know you suffered from Schizophrenia."

I nod, slowly.

"We don't like to place people of your condition in prison. Also, you are a Canadian citizen, and this complicates things."

"Complicates?"

He raises his eyebrows, suddenly.

"It's complicated," he says, like the words are produced by a trombone. He pours more tea.

"I'm not sure why you did it, Mr. Zhukov. But I can imagine your reasons were good in your own head."

"At the time," I say. "I'm not sure anymore."

"Well, hindsight is 20/20."

"So I've heard."

He pauses, then sets his cup down.

"We're releasing you from prison. You will be transferred back to a mental hospital in Canada. They will have to decide how long you stay. Or rather, you will have to decide."

I move my mouth, but I don't know what to say. It's hard to believe that I'm hearing him right, or that I'm even awake.

"Now, now," he says gently to my look of astonishment. He seems to take on a calm and meditative air. "The lawyer is waiting just outside. Our men will take you to a hotel where you'll be placed under house arrest until you can be flown back."

"I understand," I say.

"Good," he says, then lets out a sigh. He sets his teacup down then moves his finger along the porcelain, thinking. When he finally speaks he's not looking at me.

"I was wondering if you could do me a favour, Mr. Zhukov. While you're in the hotel, could you write me a letter? I'll burn it after you write it, so you don't have to worry. I'd just like to know why you did it."

I nod slowly.

"I think I can do that."

He nods slowly, straying little from the gravity he possessed. He lets on a small smile. Then he looks at me with a gentler eye which turns analytical, and I don't think he knows exactly what to think of me. Finally he looks down and grips the teacup again.

"I wish you the best, Mr. Zhukov," he says. "Now, the man should be just outside the door."

I get up slowly.

"Just outside the door," he says, when I pause at the handle.

I knock. I hear keys in the lock before the door swings wide. Three guards stare blankly at me, clothed in green uniforms, straight-backed and ready for action but calm. Standing behind them is an East Indian man, poking his balding head over the fray. When he spots me, he looks at me with a smile and our eyes meet. I see compassion.

"Stand back please," the man in the suit says, motioning with his hands for the guards to relax. "Please stand back. He's probably not dangerous."

He politely extends his hand to me.

"I'm Michael Ignano," he says with a short nod. "If you'll come with me we'll get this all sorted out, Mr. Zhukov."

We start walking with an escort, moving slowly along the halls. We take a left at the corner, away from the door which leads to the prison yard, then continue quickly past a number of rooms with steel doors and painted numbers. We halt at a green door which leads to the parking lot. A guard fumbles in the lock. The bolt slips out. He swings the door wide as a chauffeur would. Outside is blue sky and a wind blows in. I have to imagine it is a greater freedom than the kind I'd find here amongst dust. I move my feet—taking a step towards the light—when the lawyer puts a hand on my shoulder.

"It's going be alright now, Mr. Zhukov. I'm gonna make sure you're alright."

And just like that, I'm out into the sky.

PART IV:
EPILOGUE

I had this idea for drug testing on human beings. But then I forgot it. I thought I had it all figured out but then some other piece of logic just came along and knocked it over. It was really fucked up, pardon my language, Doc, but it was, yeh know? Like you just can't wrap your head around it. They were always just flapping and buzzing in there. It was a real mess. I'm telling you, the whole idea of trying to help someone is always fraught with challenge. Especially when you try to help someone too quickly, instead of going the whole extra mile. Oh, we could probably just ship in enough antibiotics. I mean, we're just doing our duty right? How much praise can we expect? To those who are given much, much is expected I suppose. So we blame every person who gives money for the wrongs which occur. That's not fair at all! I wanted to help too! I wanted to do my part. But then you see what came of it all. It was just a huge fucking disaster. And in the end I ended up maybe worse than before. That's choice for you! Choice. It leads every which way. If something goes wrong in this world when you're a politician they'll say you made the wrong choice. But that's not it at all. Many choices are fraught with uncertainty. At least the uncertain choices.

It's alright, Zhukov.

You can just call me John. I haven't been called John in a while.

Alright, John. Do you think about these things often?

Only when I'm alone and all. I had a lot of time to think about it when they had me holed up in that place. That prison was pretty disgusting.

I mean, if you want to fix the country you can always start with the prisons. That's something which isn't uncertain. Prisons everywhere are just awful.

You said there was an incident in the prison as well.

Yeh. I don't like seeing the dead dishonoured. So I sort of intervened. I think I must be going really crazy Doc. I've been doing that a lot lately and I was getting really angry for a while. But I'm feeling a better now. I got that part under control.

When did the anger start?

It was while I was working at that horrible hospital. Let me tell you, it was really a dump. I mean some of it wasn't so bad. But it could have been better, yeh know?

And when was it you say this fire started?

I don't know. I hardly remember it.

I see.

I have memory problems, Doc.

I'm aware. But you alluded before that this wasn't the first fire.

No. There was another one. I remember something about that. I'm not really sure what happened completely. There was an incident in the clinic. That's what they called it. They never caught the guy. Kind of pathetic really if you ask me. They said it must have been people from outside the clinic, come to start trouble and all.

And you remember nothing of it? Who might have started it?

I remember we were all cleared out. Everyone was moved out until the fire was put out.

An interesting concept.

It was a bit of a scare. I remember going home early that day. I wasn't supposed to, but I did. It was pretty messed up.

Is there a reason you feel you need to write everything down?

In case I don't remember it. It's kind of lame, I know. But in case I come up with something later which might be helpful.

I suppose that seems prudent. Where do you plan on living now?

I'll be staying at a hotel until I go back home. I'm moving back to Montreal. I can't stay here anymore. Not after what happened.

Do you have family there?

I used to.

None now?

Not anymore. It was just me and my mother for the longest time. Now it's only me.

What is your take on what you've been through, Zhukov?

My take? Take your pick! The field of psychology has been a mixture of paganism and science. A neo-paganism evolving from random delusion by men who professed and were professed by others to have superior insight into the inner workings of flawed man's brain. Is it any wonder that many regard some psychology to be on equal footing with alchemy and astrology? But enough real science remains in order for the field to survive and maintain an almost complete credibility within some circles, where it should have been separated into fact and fiction by real, objective scientists. You need to know first, this is the way I feel about it, doctor. I don't mean to disparage, but I'm not sure what to say about this whole thing I've been subjected to. Even in hard science with a scientific method, fraud and pseudo-religious belief still maintain a foothold. How much more then, in the field of psychology? Where it's hard to prove anything wrong. Where you can just make things up? But look at me! Look at all the work I need done. And obviously, painstakingly, slowly, you doctors have been able to figure me out. A little bit here. A delusion there. Sociology is fairly strong. The experiments—while possibly unethical—produce results.

What do you plan to do now that you know you're going to be discharged from the mental ward today?

I don't know. I want to visit my mother's grave. I haven't been there in a while.

Do you think you'll contact us if you need more help?

Yes. Now that I'm in Canada I will. Things just got kind of messed up for a while. It's a lot easier to make choices here.

I can see what you mean. Do you think the judge made the right decision in clearing you of all charges?

I don't know, Doc. I still don't know about that. I just hope that I can live with myself now. I'm sorry for what I did. Boy, am I sorry. These choices seemed like the problem before. But now I realize it's the fact that I'm flawed and don't have absolute wisdom that I can't figure out how to make those choices when they come along. It's the flaw which is the problem. It started the day I saw Jimmy Canelop behind the dumpster with Julia. It started with the anarchy of immoral chaos. What it means to be a human who lacks absolute wisdom. What separates flawed man from the animals. I was the problem and flawed man was the problem. We all are, and I still am.